Princess Asha and the Lost City of Shambhala

by

Lisa Margaret Bishop

Princess Asha and the Lost Cities

Book 1

The Lost City of Dwarka

Book 2

The Lost City of Shambhala

Be sure to check out our Facebook page 'Princess Asha and The Lost Cities'

www.princessasha.com

For information contact

author@princessasha.com

First printed edition September 2018

ISBN: 978-1-9996020-5-5

Disclaimer: This is a work of fiction. Names, characters, businesses, places, events, locales, and incidents are either the products of the author's imagination or used in a fictitious manner. Any resemblance to actual persons, living or dead, or actual events is purely coincidental.

Dedication

I dedicate this book to:

My rock, my husband, Gavin Bishop, who believes in me and supports me in my writing.

To Anthony Mahabir, who continues to teach me the path to enlightenment. Anthony has been my strength throughout my spiritual enlightenment and my life has not been the same since.

To my friends who have been with me from the beginning, Melissa Mahabir, Ella Gerassimova, Dipa Gore, Angela and Paul Wright.

To Clarice Mahabir for being my first young reader.

Table of Contents

Prologue

It was a dark, starry night and the air was warm and still in the Thar desert. It was so quiet, that the voices of men talking inside an ancient fort could be heard from miles away. As their camels stood outside waiting for their masters, the voices argued over the value of a flute found at the bottom of the ocean near the newly risen city of Dwarka.

"This is the flute of Krishna," an elderly man in the group said.

"This flute has magical powers. I saw it myself when the princess called upon the Sea God," he continued.

The evil king of Marwar held the flute in his hands, knowing exactly the significance of what this greedy old man had found.

"I will give you one silver coin for the flute," said the evil king.

"That flute is worth a lot more than a silver coin," the greedy old man replied to the king, pointing at the flute.

“If you value your life old man, I would take the coin and walk away,” the evil king replied.

Before the old man could say another word, the king looked over at his guard, and nodded. The guard grabbed the old man by the arm and threw him down the steps of the ancient fort.

The king watched the old man fall towards his camel and shouted out,

“Never return to Marwar again.”

He threw the silver coin in the old man’s general direction and walked away, laughing with his guard as he tucked the flute into his belt.

The greedy old man climbed onto his camel feeling angry and cheated as he started his journey back to Gujarat.

As they walked through the desert, the sand dunes began to shake. It looked like water was rising from beneath the sand.

The camel, sensing danger, dropped onto its knees and rolled over.

The old man fell from the camel's back. The camel seized the opportunity and ran as fast as it could, leaving the old man behind.

The greedy old man tried to run after his camel, but could not keep up.

"Wait, please don't leave me," he called out. The camel kept on running, ignoring the calls of its former master.

The water rising from under the sand was becoming deeper and flowing with a strong current.

From nowhere, part of the desert had become a gushing river. The water gripped the old man and pulled him down-stream.

He was never seen again, a fitting punishment for his greed.

As quickly as it had risen, the river disappeared and returned back to the sandy desert it had been moments earlier.

The evil king of Marwar arrived back at his palace with the flute. He took it into his quarters and locked it away, out of reach from any would-be thieves.

This flute could be the key to overthrowing other kingdoms, he thought to himself. *I could become the ruler of all of India.*

He left his quarters laughing as he walked along the hallways of his palace.

Chapter 1 - The Dream

Princess Asha of Panchala was walking through a beautiful meadow surrounded by a futuristic city; the water looked white and the palaces were made of crystals.

She could hear a voice calling to her.

“Asha, it is time my child,” the voice said gently.

"Asha, it is time for you to come," the voice said again.

Asha was trying to work out where the voice was coming from. It sounded like it was emanating from all around her. She stood in the tall green grass of the beautiful meadow looking around.

Suddenly, a hand grabbed her shoulder from behind.

Asha jumped to see who it was, but when she looked, she found herself sitting up in her bed sweating from anxiety.

This was the third dream during which she had found herself in this same city. The same voice continued to call her, as it had done over the past two weeks since her return from Gujarat.

Asha got out of bed and dressed for breakfast. It was Prince Emir of Gujarat's last day of his royal visit to the kingdom of Panchala. The King and Queen, Asha's parents, insisted on having a breakfast celebration before his journey back home.

Princess Asha had become very close to Prince Emir during his two week stay and was sad to see him leave. As she walked outside into the gardens, the prince was already waiting for her.

"Good morning Asha," Emir said, bowing to the princess. "I hope that you slept well," he continued.

"Actually, I would like to speak with you about that," Asha replied.

"You would like to speak with me about how well you slept?" Emir said scratching his head and sounding confused.

Asha hooked her arm into Emir's and they walked through the beautiful gardens filled with colorful flowers and plants.

As they walked away from the crowd of people gathering to have breakfast, Asha told Emir about the recurring dreams that she had been having since she arrived home.

"This is the third dream in two weeks. It's the same dream repeating itself and I'm really concerned," Asha said, gazing at Emir with her big brown eyes.

"It feels so real, as if I'm actually standing in this paradise kingdom, with palaces made of crystals. Suddenly, somebody grabs onto my shoulder from behind. I never get to see who it is, because I wake up as soon as I turn around."

Asha was starting to feel a little bit crazy as she heard herself talking about her dreams out loud.

Emir stood silently.

Asha was starting to regret sharing her dreams and waited for Emir to burst into laughter.

After what felt like an eternity of waiting, Asha spoke again.

"You think I'm crazy, that's why you won't say anything," she said, throwing her arms up in the air. "Let's go back and have some breakfast, before you decide that you never want to see me again."

Asha was feeling frustrated and turned to walk towards the crowd.

Emir grabbed hold of her hand.

"Wait, I'm sorry Asha. I'm a little speechless," Emir said, pulling the princess back around to face him. "The crystal cities haven't been spoken of in thousands of years. I don't understand why you would be having dreams about them," he said with a mixture of excitement and fear in his voice.

"What are the crystal cities?" Asha asked

"They're meant to be a myth, I don't know much about them. Much like the lost city of Dwarka, nobody ever speaks of the stories. All I know is that the only ones who can enter are said to be the pure of heart," he replied to her.

Asha took a deep breath, "That's enough about lost cities for today, let us go and have some breakfast. You have a long journey home and we don't want you to starve."

Smiling at one another, they joined the others for breakfast. As everyone was seated, little Najeena decided to sneak off into the flower beds to have a feast of her own.

“Get out of there,” screamed one of the attendants, chasing Najeena with a broom across the gardens.

The Queen gave Asha a stern look.

“Asha, we have spoken about this before. Najeena needs to understand that she cannot eat the flower beds,” she said.

“I’m so sorry mother, I will make sure that she doesn’t do it again,” Asha replied, looking down with an angry glare at Najeena, as she ran to her mistress’s side. Najeena curled up on the floor next to Asha, looking sorry for herself.

Soon it was time for Prince Emir and his royal guards to journey back to Gujarat.

The King and Queen of Panchala said farewell to the prince, then left their daughter and Emir to say their goodbyes in private.

"Asha, my kingdom is always open to you. I hope that you don't wait too long to come and visit," Prince Emir said, holding onto Asha's hands whilst gazing into her eyes.

"The same goes for you Emir, my palace doors are always open to you and to your family," Asha said smiling back at the handsome prince. "You don't have to go, you can stay as long as you want," she continued, blushing at the prince.

"I wish I could stay, but I must get back to my duties in Gujarat. I will miss you very much though," Emir said as he pulled her towards him.

The prince stared at the princess and decided that this would be the perfect opportunity to kiss her.

The kiss was very unexpected for Asha, but very romantic.

Asha stood at the gates and watched her handsome prince depart. Asha knew that she was falling in love with Emir as she watched him leave on his horse.

She sat down next to Najeena on the grand steps of the courtyard, already feeling sad and lonely.

"What are we going to do now Najeena?" Asha said with a sad voice. "I know! Let's go and visit

Aadesh. We haven't had the chance to visit him since we have been back,"

Asha felt a little happier knowing that she wouldn't be so lonely after all.

Asha and Najeena headed over the pastures and into the barn where Aadesh spent most of his time.

When they walked in, Aadesh was cleaning out the stalls, getting ready to feed the cows. He looked up when he heard Najeena's hooves trotting in and saw Asha following behind.

"Princess Asha, Namaste. How are you?" Aadesh said while giving Najeena a cuddle.

"I am well, thank you Aadesh, you are looking well also. Can I ask you a question please?" Asha asked.

"Of course, Your Highness, anything," Aadesh replied.

Asha stood silently for a few seconds, not quite sure how to speak without sounding crazy.

"What is it Asha?" he asked. "You look very concerned about something," Aadesh continued.

"Have you ever heard of the crystal cities?" Asha asked.

"Do you mean the crystal cities of which Shambhala is the capital city?" asked Aadesh.

"To be honest, I'm not quite sure," Asha answered. "I keep having a recurring dream of me standing in this beautiful city, with beautiful palaces made from millions of crystals. There is always a soft gentle voice speaking to me. A person grabs me by the shoulder and when I turn around, I wake up," Asha explained.

"Shambhala hasn't been spoken of in many, many years. No-one has ever been able to find this city, although many people have tried," Aadesh said. "It is said that only the gods and the pure of heart can enter," he continued.

"Why would I be having these dreams?" Asha asked.

Aadesh looked at Asha blankly, not knowing what to say to her. His face broke into a smile, "Come and have some food, I have made plenty," he said.

As Asha followed Aadesh out of the barn and headed to his home, she felt confused.

Why didn't he answer me? Aadesh knows everything, she thought to herself. *Why won't he answer my question?*

Asha decided to stop talking about her dreams and to talk about her amazing adventure to Gujarat instead.

Chapter 2 - The Flute

Back in the kingdom of Marwar, the tyrant king was working on his plan. He was somehow going to find the lost city of Shambhala, and strengthen his stature and coffers using the treasures within.

The king's ancestors had left a map inside the walls of his ancient palace, which held the secret location of the entrance to Agartha, the 'inner earth'.

This was the continent for which Shambhala was the capital city.

The king knew that it had been impossible for him to enter into Agartha, because he was neither a god, nor pure of heart.

Now though, he had possession of the flute of Krishna.

The legends spoke of how the music from this flute would open the entrance to this city and to other lost cities. All he needed to do was learn how to play this sacred instrument

With the stories that were told by his ancestors over the thousands of years, the tyrant king knew that the crystal cities were special and unique.

Shambhala was said to be home to many jewels, crystals and gold. Even the water was said to be magical.

The cities were said to be thousands of years advanced, with innovations and technologies that the outside world had never seen. The king believed that if he could gain access to all of this, and was able to steal the gold and jewels from the inner earth, he would be able to rule over the entire world.

However, what the king didn't know, was that these cities were protected by the gods.

The tyrant king gathered his men to prepare for the journey ahead.

He wanted his men to be clear that they needed to take whatever actions were necessary to enter Agartha. They were to plunder its secrets, even if such actions led to war.

"Gather all of your weapons and sharpen your swords," the king shouted to his men, "We will destroy anything or anyone that gets in our way," he continued.

The king tried to play the flute one more time, but still no notes could be heard. He packed the flute into his bag and turned to one of his guards.

"We need to make a stop in Panchala," the evil king said to his guard with a grin. "There is somebody there that I need to bring with us, to help us get into Shambhala."

The next morning, in the kingdom of Panchala, princess Asha was trying to find any literature on the crystal cities in the royal library.

Asha needed to know more about these cities, in particular Shambhala, to understand why she was dreaming about it.

As Asha read through the books, she came across some loose papers that looked like the beginnings of an unfinished manuscript. Asha pulled the papers out from the shelf.

That's strange, why would anybody put unfinished works on the shelf? She thought to herself.

Asha read through the papers to see what they were about. The first few pages were drawings of a crystalline palace with surrounding waterfalls. There were bridges across those waterfalls which led out onto beautiful meadows, full of green grass and flowers.

This is what I saw in my dreams, Asha thought. She sat on a chair and continued her review of the papers to see if she could find any more clues about this magnificent city and why it was haunting her.

As she flicked through the pages, the princess saw writings about how the pure of heart and the gods took refuge in an underground world to escape the evil of Kali Yuga, the beginning of the dark age. These people journeyed into the depths of the earth and built cities from crystals. The writings said that the water was so pure, it appeared to be white to the naked eye. The final notes said that the gods would watch from below, as the world above would destroy itself from greed, hatred and ego.

Can all of this be true? Even after raising Dwarka, has mankind still lost its purity because of power and greed? Asha asked herself.

The book was never finished, and there was nothing left to read.

Asha knew where she might get some answers.

She called for Najeena and headed over the hills to the farm to go and see if her wise friend Aadesh knew anything about these new writings.

It was a beautiful day, with flowers blooming and bees buzzing in the fields. All of the cows were grazing in the pastures, but Aadesh was nowhere to be found.

Asha went over to his house to see if he was there but could not find him.

She could only think of one other place he might be, so they headed for the lake on the other side of his pastures.

As she approached the top of the grassy hill, Asha could see Aadesh in the distance meditating, without a care for the world around him.

"You always look so peaceful when you meditate," Asha said as she sat down beside him.

“You promised to teach me how to do this,” she said with a large grin on her face.

“I’m here whenever you are ready, Your Highness,” Aadesh replied, “Rule number one, never sneak up on a person who is in deep meditation,” he said with a chuckle.

“My goodness, I’m so sorry,” Asha said, worried that he was upset with her.

“It’s fine Asha, I was about to finish anyway,” Aadesh said, putting his hand on her shoulder to assure her that he was not upset.

“To what do I owe the pleasure of your presence and that of young Najeena?” he asked, “By the way, has

Najeena stopped growing?" he said quickly before Asha had answered his first question.

"To be honest I haven't really paid any attention, I thought her height was normal at this age," Asha answered.

"Najeena should be much bigger by now, I'm thinking that she might be a dwarf cow," said Aadesh.

"She is really cute this size and I love her just the way she is," Asha said hugging Najeena.

"That is as you wish then," Aadesh replied chuckling, "Although I'm sure that your visit is not about dwarf cows. There seems to be something weighing on your mind."

"I can't stop thinking about my dreams. They have to be more than just dreams, they must be a message of some sort," She paused, "As I raised Dwarka, the Sea God told me that there was more to come, that I had not finished my quest. Maybe this is a sign," explained Asha.

"Unfortunately, this is part of your journey that you will have to figure out on your own Princess Asha. I'm afraid that I do not know much about the crystal cities, other than that which I have already told you" he replied.

"There is something that I do have that I can give to you though. Let's go back to the barn," Aadesh got up and helped Asha to stand.

Najeena ran off into the pastures with the other cows. Aadesh and Asha headed into the barn.

Aadesh reached for a key, hidden behind one of the barn doors. He went over to his desk, unlocked a drawer, and pulled out a very old looking piece of paper.

"I thought about sharing this with you on your last visit. It has been in my family for many generations. It was never discussed openly and was always kept locked away," Aadesh said as he walked over to Asha to hand it to her.

"What is it?" Asha asked as she opened it.

"It is a map. It is meant to be one of the entrances to Agartha, the underworld or inner earth as some call it. This is where most people believe

Shambhala is located. Unfortunately some of the map has faded away and not all can be seen," answered Aadesh.

"Many evil leaders have tried to find the entrance to this mystical world and all have failed. It is really difficult to locate because the entrance is hidden in the center of the Himalayan mountains," he continued.

"Are you holding any other family heirlooms in secret that I should know about now Aadesh?" Asha asked, thinking herself funny. Aadesh said nothing but smiled.

"Only the pure of heart can enter the inner world, my child," a familiar voice said from behind. It was the old lady from the village, standing at the entrance of the barn with her walking stick.

"You know what we are talking about?" questioned Asha.

"It is time for the princess to know of her next quest, Aadesh," the old lady said as she hobbled into the barn to sit down. "It is time for her to receive the sword of righteousness, the Nandaka sword."

"The Nandaka sword? I now have to carry around a bladed weapon?" Asha asked sarcastically.

"It is the sword that once belonged to Krishna," said Aadesh as he went into the stable, to the place that he had once kept the flute. He pulled out a sword that was wrapped in a gold piece of material.

“I was joking Aadesh!” said Asha. “What am I supposed to do with a sword?” she asked, feeling very concerned, “Please tell me that I don’t have to use this?”

The old lady spoke, “Asha, my child, you are pure of heart, the chosen one. It is only you that can enter Agartha. You are the only one who will be welcomed into the crystal city of Shambhala,” she paused and lowered her voice, “You must deliver this sword to the king of Shambhala, the sword will stay there to await the birth of Kalki,” she continued.

“Who is Kalki?” Asha asked, and Aadesh replied.

“Kalki will be the destroyer of all evil. When mankind has become so selfish and greedy and has completely lost all sense of love and kindness, Kalki will come to end the Kali Yuga age.”

"Please explain why I bothered to travel to the west coast to call upon the Sea God if we are all doomed anyway?" Asha asked angrily. "I thought the whole reason for raising Dwarka was to help people to remember who we truly are, and where we came from. Now you are telling me that the world is going to get worse?"

The old lady paused and replied,

"The prophecy says that the world will be controlled by tyrants and evil. No one will believe in the creators anymore and they will become myths. Mankind will resort to stealing, murder and greed. Their hunger for power will destroy earth. It is your destiny to prevent this from happening princess. The future can change if we can start believing and learn the true meaning of love again,".

"Unconditional love? That's it?" Asha asked. "If it's that simple, then why don't the people just love one-another?"

"Over thousands of years, mankind has chosen the love of material things instead of love for one another. The more mankind has had, the more they have wanted. The love of greed itself and power from material items has started to change people. It has made us forget the real reason of why we are here. Mankind created evil in the world and because of this, our karma will one day be our doom," said the old lady in a sad voice.

“You say that a lot,” Asha said, her voice again laced with sarcasm.

“This is not a joking matter princess; the future does not look bright. In fact, it looks very dark. Our karma and the way that we are treating mother earth will cause many catastrophes. We will be controlled by greedy groups of men, dictators who won’t listen to the people. We will lose all of our rights to free speech and the way that we have chosen to live,” warned the old lady.

“What if I am not let into Agartha?” asked Asha.

“You will be, you are expected. These dreams are your calling, they are real, Asha,” explained the old lady.

"You need to take the flute and play it at the entrance to Agartha. The music will open the falling waters for you to enter," said the old lady.

"About the flute," interrupted Asha, "I don't actually know where it is. It went missing the night that the Sea God raised Dwarka," She was feeling uneasy as the old lady and Aadesh stared at her incredulously.

The three of them stood staring at each other for what seemed like an eternity but was really only minutes. They were staring at each other in an awkward silence, until one of Asha's palace guards came running into the barn.

Trying to catch his breath, he called out to the princess,

"Princess Asha, Princess Asha, I need to speak with you urgently."

"What is it? Whatever has happened?" Asha asked, concerned by the look on his face.

"Your Highness, we just received word that the King of Marwar is on his way here with all of his army to kidnap you," the guard replied, gulping on his words anxiously.

"The King of Marwar! What would he want with me?" Asha asked looking back at Aadesh.

"We captured one of his soldiers. He speaks of a map that the king holds to a secret magical city, hidden in the mountains. This map was passed to him by his ancestors. He has a sacred flute from Dwarka that he needs you to play so that he can get past the city entrance," said the guard looking at the princess wide-eyed.

"Well, I guess that answers the question as to where the flute is," said Asha, "What am I going to do?" she thought out loud. "I can't defeat a crazy king and his huge army that is twice the size of our kingdom."

"Events are unfolding as they have been foreseen for many, many years," said the old lady.

There was silence again for a several minutes.

Asha broke the silence.

"I will head to the mountains first. If he wants me, he will have to come and find me," she said.

"Your Highness, you cannot defeat this tyrant King by yourself. You will need an army," said the concerned guard.

Aadesh spoke, "Asha, you must understand that you cannot harm anyone. If you do, your heart will no longer be pure, and you will not be able to enter into the inner world."

He put his hands onto her shoulders, so that he could look at the princess, directly into her large brown eyes.

"I killed a huge serpent and my heart is still pure," said Asha.

"The serpent was a demon," said Aadesh, "It is different. The king is a man, he wasn't born evil, he chose that path for himself. Harming a man, no matter how evil he may be, goes against all the rules of unconditional love," he continued.

"I'm heading to the Himalayas at sunrise tomorrow, without an army. I'm not putting any of our people in danger, just because I was careless and lost the flute. It is my fault that it is in the hands of this tyrant king," Asha said, looking directly at the guard.

Aadesh covered the sword in the gold cloth and handed it to Asha. She said her goodbyes to the old lady and hugged her friend.

As Asha and the guard left the barn, the old lady hobbled over to her.

She grabbed onto Asha's hands and said, "remember my child, love conquers all."

Asha, Najeena and the guard headed back to the palace. The first part of Asha's plan was to tell her parents that she had to go on another adventure.

As she walked into the throne room to speak with her parents, all she thought to herself was, *this isn't going to be easy. I am sure that there will be lots of tears.*

As Asha walked up to the king and queen, the tears came just as she expected. "Father, I haven't even said anything yet, you can't let your people see you cry," Asha said embarrassed by her father's emotions.

"Mother, please can you get him under control, this is embarrassing," she muttered to the queen.

The queen smiled at Asha and walked over to her daughter,

“Sweetheart, a parent will never get used to their child departing.” The queen kissed Asha on her forehead, “give your father a hug goodbye and I will help you pack for your journey.”

While the queen and Asha were packing necessities for the princess’ travels, the queen looked at Asha, wondering what she was thinking about.

“Asha my child, what is wrong? Why do you look so sad?” asked the queen.

“I can’t stop thinking about this king and his army. What if he defeats me? What if I can’t get the flute from him?" Asha asked, looking at her mother, both of their eyes filling up with tears.

"Asha my darling sweet child, if anybody can do this, it is you. You are the strongest person I have ever known. This is not because of the strength of your body, but because of the strength of your heart. These men might be physically strong on the outside with large muscles, but you hold the biggest one of all on the inside. When you listen with your heart, you will always win," said the queen, hugging her daughter.

"There is a big possibility that I may not conquer these men mother, then nobody will believe in me anymore. I will have failed my people, I will have failed you and father," Asha said looking up at her mother with a tear rolling down her cheek.

“Asha my child, the only way that people will stop believing in you, is when you stop believing in yourself. Trying is not failing, giving-up is failing. I know that you can do this, it is your destiny!” the queen said holding onto Asha’s face.

“Come, you need to get a good night of sleep before you leave in the morning,” said the queen. She tucked her daughter into bed and kissed her on the forehead.

“Mother?” Asha called out as the queen was just about to leave her room.

“Yes, my darling,” replied the queen as she turned around.

"Will you look after Najeena for me while I'm gone please? I cannot take her this time. It is too dangerous," Asha said.

The queen nodded her head with a smile and left Asha to sleep.

Chapter 3 - Journey to the Mountains

The sun was rising, and Asha was ready to start yet another quest for the good of mankind.

Before she mounted her horse, Spirit, she said her goodbyes to her parents and to Najeena.

“You be a good girl while I’m gone, Najeena,” Asha said, hugging her little cow.

Asha hugged her parents and then jumped up onto Spirit. As Asha was trying to get up onto his back, she could feel herself being pulled downwards. When Asha looked down to see what was pulling her away from her saddle, she saw that it was Najeena, grabbing onto her satchel to try and stop her from leaving.

"Najeena, I have to go. I'm sorry but I can't take you this time, it's too dangerous," Asha said as she petted Najeena on the head to comfort her. Najeena stepped back and allowed the princess to get onto her horse. As she trotted out of the palace, the princess looked back to wave goodbye to a very sad looking gathering and to her little cow.

Asha trotted through the markets, greeting her people as they poked their heads out of their windows and doors to wave goodbye to their brave princess.

Word gets out fast, Asha though to herself.

Asha proceeded onto the pastures and galloped through the fields. As they approached the small lake near Aadesh's farm, Asha could see him in the distance meditating peacefully.

Asha and Spirit headed over the hills and raced on out of sight.

There was a lot for Asha to think about as she rode towards the Himalayan mountains. She had at least two days head-start before the King of Marwar would catch-up to her. Asha had to prepare herself for this tyrant king.

Her main focus was to retrieve Krishna's flute and run to the entrance of Agartha as quickly as she could.

The question she kept asking herself was *how am I going to get the flute?*

It felt like a lifetime ago, but Asha remembered what the ten-headed serpent had said about Mount Kailash on her last adventure.

I can go to the top of Kailash, the king can't get through the sacred part of the mountain, because he is not pure of heart, Asha thought to herself.

Asha headed for Mount Kailash, but she needed a way to guarantee that the evil king would find her. Asha looked around to see how she could leave a trail for him to see. She needed the king to follow her up to the top of the mountain.

Asha dismounted Spirit and took out the Nandaka sword.

She walked over to a large rock, which was set deep into the earth, and started to carve words into the rock using the sword.

She wrote:

IF YOU WANT ME, YOU WILL HAVE TO COME AND GET ME AT THE TOP OF MOUNT KAILASH.

Asha wrapped the sword back up in the cloth, climbed back onto Spirit, and headed for the mountain.

Everything felt so familiar to Asha as she rode through the quiet fields of the Himalayas. It only seemed like yesterday when the owl flew out of the forest to join her on her quest to raise Dwarka. Asha missed her feathered friend and wished that she had her by her side on this journey to Shambhala.

After a day of travelling, it was time to give Spirit a rest for the night. Asha set-up camp near a lake so that they could both drink some water and freshen up.

It was starting to get dark. Asha pulled out her blanket to lie on and tried to get some sleep. As she lay out the blanket, she realized that it had been made by a little girl from the village at the bottom of Mount Kailash. The memory of this child came clearly to Asha.

I must visit the villagers and pay my respects before I head up the mountain, thought Asha.

The princess lay on her warm blanket, gazing up at the bright stars. She thought to herself, *if only it could be this peaceful and beautiful everywhere.*

Asha couldn't understand how people could hold so much greed and hatred in their hearts.

Why do material things hold so much significance in a person's life, when mother nature holds so much more beauty than anything you can wear or trade? She thought to herself.

She started to count the stars until her eyelids felt heavy and finally she fell into a deep sleep.

The princess found herself in a field of beautiful flowers, with bees buzzing next to a stream. A familiar feminine voice was calling to Asha again. Asha had heard this voice before, but knew that she had never met this person.

"Asha, Asha you must protect the sword from evil. The Nandaka sword must stay in the hands of purity," the gentle voice said. "You must not let anyone follow you to the entrance of Agartha," the voice continued.

Asha looked around to see who was talking. The voice was so beautiful that it sounded like music when the mysterious woman spoke. This magical kingdom was so mesmerizing and peaceful that Asha didn't want to leave. There was no negative energy, just a sense of happiness and peace.

Princess Asha didn't want to leave the meadow, she wanted to see the person talking to her. She felt a hand grabbing at her shoulder again.

"You must wake up Asha. You need to reach the top of the mountain before the king of Marwar reaches you," the voice said to her.

The princess turned around to see if the woman was still behind her. As she turned around she realized that it was Spirit nudging her shoulder.

Another dream, Asha thought to herself. *This time it felt more real than before.*

The sun was beginning to rise, then Asha's stomach started rumbling.

"I'm so hungry I could eat a horse," Asha said out loud.

Spirit looked up at Asha, whilst taking a drink from the lake, and grunted at her.

"Sorry Spirit, I didn't mean it literally," Asha said with a guilty and awkward smile. "I would never really eat a horse! Let's head to the village, maybe the pilgrim villagers will be kind enough to give us a meal," Asha said as she climbed onto his back.

It was a long morning of travel and Asha's stomach was really growling. She was hoping for a good home cooked meal instead of eating stale bread and cheese. Asha was getting excited, she could see the little village in the distance.

She was looking forward to having some good wholesome food and good conversation before heading up Mount Kailash.

As Asha rode into the village, the pilgrims ran up to her, excited to see their heroine princess once again.

They knew that this time, she would have many stories to share about her last adventure. The children gathered around her as she climbed down from Spirit. They were grabbing at her and begging for tales of Dwarka.

“Okay, okay little ones. Give the princess some space,” a voice said from behind. “Your Highness, you must be starving. Let’s take you inside for some food.”

It was the beautiful wife of the village chief. She took Asha by the arm, smiling at her as they pushed their way through the excited children.

Asha breathed in deeply through her nose, enjoying the delicious smells of the freshly made food that was already prepared on the table. She sat down at the table ready to eat.

As the food was being put in front of her, the princess looked up at the chief’s wife.

“I cannot take Spirit with me on the rest of my journey. Would somebody be so kind as to return him to the palace for me please?" she asked with a mouthful of food.

"It would be an honor, Your Highness," the lady said looking at Asha and trying not to chuckle at her. The princess was eating as if this was her first meal in months.

"You must have been really hungry Princess Asha," the lady said as she collected the soon empty plate.

"I was starving. Thank you so much for your generosity and kindness," Asha said, gulping down her cup of water.

"We have packed some fresh fruit and bread for your travels," said the chief's wife. "Please be safe, this king is not a person to be underestimated," she continued.

Asha took the wrapped-up food and put it into her satchel. She looked up at the woman, staring at the fear in her eyes. Asha wasn't too sure what to say or do, it was an awkward moment that she just wanted to be over.

"I will go and say goodbye to Spirit," Asha said, turning to head out of the door.

"Your Highness, please tell me that you will be cautious when you face the King of Marwar," the woman said.

"Bodhi, is that your name?" Asha asked. The woman nodded and waited for Asha to continue.

"I fear this king more than I fear the demons that I have had to face in the past. He is a tyrant and will stop at nothing for power and greed, but this is my destiny. I will do everything in my power to fulfil this fate that has been bestowed upon me. I will not let my people down. Good conquers all!" said Asha standing tall and confident.

Bodhi walked up to the princess and gave her a big hug, "Please be safe, we are all confident that you will succeed."

Asha left the house to go and say goodbye to Spirit and the rest of the villagers. She stood in front of all who were gathered and gave a little speech.

"I want to let you all know how much I cherish your hospitality and kindness. This is the reason that I fight for my people and for humanity. Love is the strongest, most powerful weapon that mankind could have. We will conquer the darkness as long as we have the power of love."

All of the villagers cheered for Asha and she turned and smiled at Bodhi. She grabbed her satchel with the sword and headed toward Mount Kailash. All of the children followed behind her until she approached the bottom of the mountain.

Asha started to climb up and the children waved goodbye, still cheering for their heroine.

Chapter 4 - Mount Kailash

It was getting dark as the sun was setting behind the mountains. The temperature was dropping, and Asha knew that she must be at least half-way up the mountain.

It was starting to get too dark to continue walking, so the tired princess decided to call it a night and to have some rest.

It felt like déjà vu as she pulled out her blanket to wrap around herself, providing protection from the cold, damp air. This time though, Asha was all alone without her animal friends.

The princess was feeling more vulnerable, knowing that she didn't have anybody by her side to comfort her, and to warn her of any dangers whilst she slept.

Reminiscing whilst feeling a little sad and lonely, Asha closed her eyes and fell asleep.

Down in the village below, all of the people were fast asleep. It was normally very tranquil and quiet in the middle of the night, so the sound of horses trotting through the village was very unusual.

Bodhi and her husband, the Chief, awoke at the same time when they heard dozens of horses. They looked at each other, climbed out of bed and went to the entrance of their cottage to see who was coming through their land.

When they looked outside, they could see a roof on fire. They both ran out to see what was causing such chaos.

The streets echoed with screams of the villagers as they ran from their homes, scared of the fire.

Sitting on his horse in the middle of the village was the King of Marwar and his army of men, many of whom were holding fire-lances.

"What are you doing in my village?" the chief asked the king, trying to look as strong as he could muster.

"Hand over the princess and no harm will come to you or your people. If you do not hand her over, we will torch every home in your puny village," said the tyrant king with an evil smirk on his face.

"We are not afraid of you," said Bodhi forcing herself in front of her husband. "Princess Asha is also not afraid of you," Bodhi continued angrily.

The king laughed and shouted back, "Where is she then? Why hasn't she shown herself to me?"

"She is not here, she is waiting for you at the top of Mount Kailash," the chief said as he pulled his wife behind him, out of harm's way.

"In that case, I suppose we had better not keep the little miss waiting," said the king laughing aloud with his men.

As the invading army proceeded deeper into the village to get through to the other side, two of the guards lit two more roofs on fire. They cantered off on their horses, laughing evilly with their king.

The pilgrims rushed to bring as many buckets of water as they could carry to help put out the fires. Unfortunately, one of the homes was left completely destroyed.

"It is okay my people, they are gone," the chief said. "We can rebuild tomorrow, but for now, those left without a home, please come into mine and rest," the chief continued.

The next morning at the crack of dawn, the sun was rising and so was Asha.

As the princess stood to get water and food, she could see many men climbing up the mountain with their torches and weapons. Asha realized that this must be the King of Marwar and his army.

Asha decided to eat on the move whilst hiking up the mountain. She did not want the king and his men to catch-up with her before she got to the sacred ground of the mountain.

I will not rest tonight, Asha thought to herself. *I will not let these men have any advantage over me.*

Every few hours, Asha stopped to take a drink and looked back to see if the men were any closer.

Wow they are moving quickly, she thought.

Asha carried on walking up and around the mountain, moving a little faster.

She had walked for hours without a proper rest and was starting to feel dizzy. The cold air was chilling and thinning the higher that she climbed. It was making it harder for her to breathe. Asha took out her bottle of water for a drink and realized that the water was becoming frozen.

Darkness was approaching, and Asha was feeling ever-more weak and tired. She had nothing to drink now, her water was completely frozen. She held onto a rock for support and pulled herself up the mountain, trying not to collapse from exhaustion.

The Princess knew that she was becoming delirious. Her teeth were chattering, and her fingers were numbed from the cold air. Asha took the blanket out of her bag and wrapped it around her shoulders to keep her warm. She didn't remember it being this cold the last time she had journeyed here.

Asha could feel that she was getting closer to the sacred part of the mountain. All of her senses were feeling out of sorts and voices were whispering inside her head.

Now, more than ever, the princess needed to concentrate on not looking back, and not giving in to the cries in her mind of her loved ones in despair.

The first voice suddenly spoke clearly. It was her mother, crying for her to return.

"Asha, I'm scared, please come back. I don't want to lose you," the voice cried out. Asha knew that this was not real. She knew that the queen was very supportive of her daughter's quest to Shambhala.

Next, she could hear Prince Emir.

"Asha, I'm in danger. Somebody is after me, I need your help, please!"

Asha stopped, closed her eyes and took in two deep breaths. She could feel the fatigue overwhelming her.

Asha had to focus to remember where she was and not give in to her exhaustion. This was just a test. She had passed it before, and knew that she would pass it again.

Asha held onto the rocky wall to pull herself around the mountain, cries for help continued ringing in her head. She decided to sing, to erase the sounds of any more voices crying out to her.

Asha sang a beautiful lullaby that her mother used to sing to her when she was a little girl to help her sleep. The loving melody helped Asha to remember who she was, and where she had come from.

Finally, Asha moved past the fog and into the light on the other side of the mountain. She was still standing on the sacred ground, but the test was finally over.

Asha's mind became clear and the air warmed up as the sun shone onto her face. The princess was able to breathe easily again. More than that, her water was thawing, so she was able to take a well-deserved drink.

Asha sat down against the rock to have a nap before she had to face the tyrant king of Marwar.

She shut her eyes and fell into a deep sleep. The princess dreamt of all her loved ones back home.

Chapter 5 - The Fight

Asha slept soundly, dreaming of her home. She could hear lots of footsteps coming closer to her in her dream. She was sitting in front of her mother who was brushing her long beautiful hair and the footsteps were getting closer and louder.

“Asha, I know that you are here. Your little friends in the village told me that you were waiting for me,” laughed the evil king.

Asha was still dreaming, but she could hear the voices.

She turned around to look at her mother, to see if the queen knew who was calling for her. With the turning movement, Asha banged her head on a rock and woke up with a start.

Those voices are real, they aren't in my dream, Asha thought to herself.

She jumped up and crept around the corner to see who was calling her name. As Asha moved past the rock, she could make out the outline of shadows of men through the fog.

Asha crept through the fog so that she could see the king clearly.

She knew that she was safe, as long as she stayed within the sacred grounds of the mountain.

With the king being so evil and greedy, he would never be able to come to where Asha was standing.

"I hear that you are looking for me, Your Highness," Asha said confidently, with faith that she was protected.

"Well look at what we have here, it's the heroic Princess Asha, the one who raised Dwarka" laughed the king.

"Hand over my flute," shouted Asha, "It doesn't belong to you."

The king of Marwar laughed and the rest of his men laughed along with him.

"Or what?" replied the king, still laughing.

"I am not afraid of you," said Asha firmly.

"Yes, I have heard that, from that feisty lady in the village," the king said mockingly. "Was it that lady's house that we burned to the ground?" the king asked his men, laughing again with them all.

Asha could feel herself turning red with rage. Hearing that her friends were in danger because of her made Asha feel very guilty.

"Why would you bring harm to innocent villagers? I am the one that you want, not them," Asha cried out.

"Yes princess, you are the one that I need, the pure of heart who will get me into Shambhala. If you do not come with me, the fate of your friends will be far worse that you can possibly imagine," threatened the king.

"Do you really believe that the entrance of Agartha will open with you by my side?" questioned Asha. "The guardians are gods, they know everything and will not be so easily fooled."

The king and his men sniggered, "I guess we shall soon see," he said.

"Do you really think that I'm going to take you to the entrance of Agartha?" asked Asha.

"Not willingly," said the king. "Capture the princess and tie her up. We don't want the little miss to run away now do we?" said the king.

Asha took out the Nandaka sword and held it in front of her. The king and his men chortled at her as she took a stance. Asha was ready to protect herself against anybody who approached her.

The king of Marwar stopped laughing and took a long hard look at the sword.

"Where did you get that sword princess?" the king asked, "that's quite a powerful weapon for a little girl."

"This sword is none of your business," Asha said.

"We will see about that, won't we?" said the king. "Seize her!" he ordered his men.

The men moved towards the princess and into the lighter fog. Suddenly one of the men dropped to his knees trying to breath, but he couldn't catch his breath and quickly fell unconscious.

Two other men took hold of their fallen comrade and pulled him back out of the fog. As he moved away from the sacred ground, he was able to catch his breath again and regain his posture.

Two more men tried to reach out to the princess, but they too fell to the ground, falling unconscious. As the men were dragged away from the fog, the king was quickly becoming furious.

"Get her," the king shouted to his men. "Are you going to let a child defeat you?"

"But your Highness, we can't get to the princess. There is some sort of curse to stop us from reaching her," said one of the king's men.

"You are all useless. I will have to do the job myself," shouted the king.

The king walked towards the fog pushing his men out of his way. As soon as he put his foot onto the sacred ground, a very loud screeching started in his ears. The noise was so unbearable that it brought him to his knees. He stepped back out of the fog, even more incensed and aggravated than before.

"If you don't come with me willingly, I will destroy the village along with all your friends within," said the king pointing down the mountainside.

"My friends are not afraid of you, so go ahead and try," Asha said in a very stern voice.

The king screamed in anger and ran towards the princess as fast as he could. The screeching in his ears got stronger and louder, but he was the only one who could hear it.

The king fell to his knees in front of Princess Asha from the unbearable pain in his ears. He looked up at Asha, begging for her to stop the curse.

"I have not put a curse on you. Whatever is happening to you is of your own doing, not mine," Asha said looking down on the king.

By this time, he was looking quite pathetic.

"You have no kindness in your heart, therefore you cannot enter the sacred ground of Mount Kailash." Asha continued.

The king continued to look up at the princess pleading for help, not understanding that it was his karma causing him pain, not Asha.

As he continued to stare at her, his eyes widened. He saw the ten-headed serpent that had helped Asha on her last journey to Mount Kailash, standing behind the princess.

"You see Your Highness, this is what happens when hatred and greed take over your heart. Love will always win, the light will always take over the darkness," Asha said.

Asha looked into his wide eyes and saw fear in them. She stood above him with the sword over his head and continued her speech, "now that I have your attention, I want you to remember this feeling and think twice about being a cruel and greedy leader."

Asha didn't realize that the serpent was hovering above her, all ten heads staring menacingly at the king. She thought that he was actually listening to her speech and feared her because of his pain!

He pointed up at the serpent but was speechless.

He crawled backwards in fear, dropping the map and the flute, clutching his ears as he tried to get out of the fog and away from the creature.

The king was so frightened by what he had seen, that he continued crawling backwards as quickly as he could.

He was not paying attention to his hazardous surroundings.

Abruptly, the ice beneath his feet collapsed and he plummeted into a deep crevasse. His screams became fainter and fainter as he fell, until soon he could no longer be heard.

Asha looked down and stared where the king had fallen, feeling sad that she could have saved him. Asha was still oblivious to the Serpent being the reason that the king fell and that it was still hovering above her head protecting her.

Asha came out of the fog and stood in front of the king's men. "I suggest to all of you, that you change your ways before you end up sharing the same fate as your king," Asha said with a strong voice and confident demeanor.

The army took one look at the giant serpent standing high above Asha and ran screaming down the mountain as quickly as they could.

Asha looked down at the blade in her hand. "Wow! I need to carry a sword around with me more often," Asha said, amazed with herself, still not knowing that the serpent had been hovering over her this whole time.

Asha went to collect the flute that the king dropped before he plummeted down the mountain. As the princess turned around, she bumped into the serpent.

Realizing that the king and his men might not have been scared of her after all, Asha asked the serpent "It was my warrior finesse, powerful words and this sword that scared them away, right?"

"It is our duty to protect you and the sacredness of this Mountain," the serpent hissed as it slithered around her feet.

"I shall take that as a yes then, one point to Asha" the princess replied.

No matter how many times the serpent saved Asha, she still wasn't comfortable with it slithering around her body like it was going to have her for lunch!

Asha walked over to pick up the flute and saw the parchment that the king had dropped lying next to it on the ground. She opened it up to see what the king had been clutching.

"The king really did have a map to Shambhala," Asha said showing it to the serpent.

"His ancestors have been trying to get into the inner world for thousands of years," said the serpent. "They have all been unsuccessful."

Asha picked up her satchel and put the flute and the map inside. She took a drink of water and splashed a little over her face.

"Thank you again for everything," Asha said to the serpent. "I must start my journey over the mountains. Now that I have this completed map, I should be able to get to Shambhala much faster."

The serpent bowed its ten heads to the princess, Asha bowed back and smiled. She headed back down Mount Kailash to continue her journey to Shambhala.

Chapter 6 - The Himalayas

Another long day had passed for Princess Asha as she journeyed through the Himalayas.

She stopped to take a look at the map that had once belonged to the King of Marwar. There were many hills and valleys in between the mountains, which made it somewhat confusing for the princess to pinpoint her location.

It looks like I have to head for Machapuchare Mountain, Asha thought to herself. *I have yet another day of walking ahead of me.*

The sun was setting, so Asha decided to get some rest. She set her blanket down on the softest part of the grass, ate some food and lay down under the stars.

It was such a beautiful clear night, with no moon, that Asha was able to see the stars clearly. As she stared up into the sky counting the stars, Asha remembered seeing some beautiful lights in the sky on the map.

Asha pulled out her map to have a look to compare it to the sky above her. The lights on the map looked exactly like the shining star path of the Milky Way that she had been staring at in the sky several nights before as well.

On the map, the stars led to the entrance of Agartha.

I guess that there is no rest for the weary, Asha thought to herself. She packed up her things and continued her journey, following the lights across the mountains.

Hours of walking passed, and the princess finally reached the first valley.

As she walked through, she could see inscriptions hidden in the rocks on both sides of the mountains. These inscriptions glowed from the brightness of the stars.

One of the drawings was a dragon bowing its huge head in respect to what looked like a giant. There was another drawing that looked like a winged elf.

Asha rubbed her eyes in disbelief at what she was seeing. *There are no such things as dragons, giants and fairies. Maybe the people who created these drawings were really bored,* Asha thought.

She continued her trek through the first valley that led out to open fields with a gushing river between the huge mountains on either side of her. There was a little village across the way. It was beautiful, quaint and so very peaceful.

Asha had never known that people lived in the valleys of the mountains. She had never realized that the valleys themselves were so vast.

The sun was rising, and Asha could see farmers coming out into the fields to feed their animals. One of the farmers looked across and stared at the princess for a moment before walking towards her. Asha decided not to be rude, so she walked towards him to introduce herself.

Before Asha could speak the farmer knelt down in front of her, bowing his head.

"Princess Asha, it would be an honor to invite you into my home and to dine with us for breakfast," said the middle-aged farmer. "Please come with me," he said as he held out his hand pointing to the direction he wanted Asha to go.

"I'm honored sir, but I really don't want to impose," Asha said feeling nervous. *How could this man know my name?* She thought.

The last village she had walked through where she was recognized, had led to villagers trying to hold her captive so that she couldn't complete her quest to the Sea God.

As she hesitantly followed the man through the long bright green grass, two little children ran up towards the farmer.

They were shouting excitedly "Papa, papa, is this really the princess?"

"Yes, my children, now please mind your manners and run along, please don't bother her Royal Highness," he quietly said to his son and daughter.

"My apologies, Your Highness, my children have heard the stories of the pure one since they were born.

It is like a fairytale come true for them to see you," the farmer said.

"It's perfectly fine, I love children," replied Asha, "By the way what did you say your name was?" she asked.

"I didn't, but my name is Jugal. Please make yourself at home, my wife is making breakfast. You must be starving," he said as he opened the door to his quaint cottage.

Asha stood at the window to look out at the village in wonder and to take-in her surroundings. It was so picturesque - Asha had never seen anything like it!

The river that ran through the valley was the purest blue. The homes were all of a good size and felt very modern. There were more than a hundred homes scattered around the valley and wild flowers grew colorfully in the green fields. The air smelled so fresh that she could just lay in the long green grass and breathe it in, all day long.

As Asha filled her lungs with a deep breath of fresh air, she could smell freshly baked bread being removed from an oven. Jugal called his children inside to prepare and had them sit quietly at the table for breakfast.

The children sat across from the princess and stared at her with big smiles on their faces. They had blueberries all around their mouths from the pre-breakfast snack that they had clearly sneaked.

Asha had to control herself to prevent her from laughing at the state that the children were in. They looked like they had eaten a bucket full of blueberries each!

As their mother took a wet cloth to wipe their mouths she scolded, “You children are going to make yourselves sick from all of the blueberries that you eat. Those blueberry trees are for the whole village, not just for the two of you.”

After a delicious breakfast, the children helped to clean up the table, whilst Jugal poured a cup of herbal tea for Princess Asha. “This tea will give you energy for the rest of your travels,” said Jugal.

"How do you know who I am?" questioned Asha

"The elders have passed on your prophecy for many generations, Your Highness. Your story has been told hundreds and hundreds of times," said Jugal.

"What story?" asked Asha.

"For centuries, a story has been told of how a young princess, the descendant of Krishna, would be born. This princess would be pure of heart, innocent and would never be judgmental. She would be the one to bring 'positive consciousness' to our world that would help get us out of Kali Yuga. She would be the only human of our time who would be allowed to enter the crystal city of Shambhala," Jugal said.

Asha sat and looked at Jugal in silence, taking all that he spoke of in.

"Um, so no pressure on me then?!" she replied and broke into a big smile at the hospitable family. *Why wouldn't Aadesh or my parents have told me about this?* She thought to herself. *Why does the whole of India seem to know more about me and my journey than I do?*

Jugal stood up from the table and asked Princess Asha to join him outside. As they walked through the fields of long grass and flowers, Jugal took them towards the river.

He sat down next to the gushing water flowing through the valley, beckoning the princess to sit next to him.

Jugal took in a deep breath through his nose and breathed out slowly through his mouth. “Do you smell that Your Highness?” He asked.

“Smell what?” Asha asked confused about what scent she should be smelling. Asha could only smell the fresh air, the freshest she has ever smelled.

“Exactly,” Jugal said with a smile. “The air is so clean and pure here. It has been foretold that in years to come, mankind will forget about nature and all of the goodness that we enjoy from the environment around us,” he said taking in a few deep breathes and continued.

“It’s the greatest gift we have ever been given from the gods, but greed for material possessions and power will take over the world. Eventually mankind will forget who we really are; how to plant our own food; the air will become unclean from man's lack of care or interest in our planet; there will be less trees and less sources of food; we will become the cause of disease; our people will not live past twenty years of age; most will die younger than that," Jugal said with a sad tone in his voice.

Asha stared into the water, trying to understand how or why anyone could ever destroy such beauty. There was so much peace and calmness in this village, she didn't want to leave.

"Why would anybody want to destroy this? I don't understand" asked Asha.

"When greed and selfishness capture our hearts and our minds, it creates a darkness, a bad energy, that is really hard to escape from," Jugal replied.

"This darkness is like a disease that takes over the body and the way that we as people think. The more that people have, the more that people will want. No amount of possessions is ever enough. That's because people's minds have been made to believe that money is power. The mindset is becoming that the more that you have, the better a person you are. Unfortunately, it is a journey that many of mankind will have to endure I'm afraid. This is the age of the Kali." said Jugal. "You can have all the riches in the world, but if you don't know peace and love, you are the poorest of them all."

"What exactly is Kali?" asked Asha, "I have heard that word a lot of late".

"Kali is a demon of greed and envy. He is currently the ruler of this world and he will stop at nothing to get into the minds of everyone that exists so that he can continue ruling the world. If Kali fails to take over the mind of man, then he can no longer exist here.

Unfortunately, he is winning the fight because mankind has started to become like Kali: greedy, envious and selfish. We are all born pure of heart, but some choose to allow Kali to take control of their souls and others choose to stay pure.

You cannot become purer, you can only become less pure. As long as we keep going on the path of impurity, we will stay in the Kali Yuga age," Jugal replied.

"Take note of that Princess Asha, you must not allow Kali to take control of your mind and soul," he added.

Asha and Jugal sat in silence for a while enjoying the sounds of the water and the birds chirping.

Suddenly they heard little giggles of a boy and a girl trying to sneak up on them. Asha and Jugal smiled at each other, pretending they couldn't hear the children.

All of a sudden, they turned around and pounced on the little ones. Asha tickled the little girl until she begged Asha to stop. The four of them stood up and headed back to the village.

After a day of tranquility, it was time for Asha to get on her way to follow the path of the Milky Way. Jugal and his family packed some fresh food and water for Asha and handed it to her before she left.

"You don't have much further to go, Your Highness. Good luck," Jugal said as he bowed down to the princess.

"Thank you for your kindness, I will never forget you, all of you," Asha said as she hugged the children goodbye.

The family stood by the door and waved goodbye to their beloved princess as she left the valley to head onto a new one.

As the sun was setting, the stars' paths were shining. Colors of blue, yellow and purple were becoming more visible for Asha to see.

As she walked between two mountains, Asha looked behind her to take one last gaze at the beautiful Himalayan valley and the village that had warmed her heart.

Chapter 7 - Topper the Elf

Asha sat on the grass in the next valley to take a break from walking.

Who knew that these mountains had so many valleys, she thought to herself.

Asha looked up to the stars and saw a bright shooting star, sweeping across the sky. She closed her eyes and made a wish.

"I wish for peace and love for my people," Asha said out loud.

"Aren't you a bit old to be making wishes on a shooting star?" a voice replied from under the rocks of the mountain.

Asha jumped up to her feet, startled by the unexpected and deep voice.

She looked all around but couldn't see anyone.

"Hello? Who's there? I demand that you show yourself," Asha said, clutching the hilt of the Nandaka sword.

"There is no need for your sword, Your Highness. You can take the princess away from her throne, but you can't take the duties of her throne away from the princess," the voice said, in a snide tone.

A pale skinned little old man with a long white beard, long white hair and pointy ears crawled out from underneath the rocks. He was about three feet tall and was holding a stick with a small bag on the end of it.

Asha put the sword down and giggled to herself. She had never seen a man so tiny before with such a confident voice.

"Are you an elf?" Asha asked.

"That is what the humans like to call us," he said, shuffling his little legs over to the princess. "Topper is my name," the elf said as he put his hand out to shake Asha's.

Asha knelt down to his level and shook his hand. She was trying not to stare too hard at Topper, but elves were always believed to be mythical in her kingdom. It was like a fairytale for Asha to actually meet a real-life elf.

“How do you know who I am?” asked Asha.

“Everybody in Agartha knows who you are, Your Highness. You are the one who is pure of heart, who raised Dwarka. There are not many unsullied folks on the outer earth anymore,” said Topper with a chuckle.

“So, you are from Agartha?” asked Asha.

“Yes, all of the elves live in Agartha,” Topper responded.

"Isn't it a little dangerous for you to be wandering around the valleys up here? Aren't you worried about someone finding and capturing you?" Asha asked.

"Humans can't see me," Topper said, standing up tall and proud.

Asha was sitting face-to-face with the elf, "I'm human and I can see you."

"Yes, but you are different. You have the gift to see things beyond the ego of a normal human being. We call those like you enlightened," said Topper.

Asha and Topper both stood quietly, staring at each other for a moment, until Topper seemingly decided that it was time for him to go.

"It was nice to meet you, Your Highness," he said, as he picked up his stick and bag and started to head through the valley.

"Wait a minute," Asha shouted out. "Can you show me the way to Agartha please?"

Topper turned around and looked up at the desperate princess and asked her, "Are you one of those princesses that likes to break into song?"

Asha looked blankly at the elf, trying to understand what his point was.

"No, I do not just break out into song, but I can if you want me to," Asha said with a wide smile on her face.

Topper grunted at Asha, "You're funny. Let's go, but no constant chit-chat, I like to walk in silence."

Asha grinned at the grumpy elf, collected her belongings and followed behind.

As they walked through the valleys of the Himalayas, the stars of the Milky Way started to disappear, and the sun began to rise.

As they moved deeper into the mountains, Asha noticed changes all around her.

The rivers sounded like music and the flowers were much bigger. They seemed to whisper to Asha as she walked by them.

There was a sense of peace and unity with nature. It was no wonder that the elf liked silence whilst walking home. There was no better sound than the voice of Mother Nature whispering quietly all around.

Topper and Asha walked for hours until they both were tired. They stopped to rest under a tree for a while.

As they sat down, Asha took out her water bottle for a long drink and offered some water to the elf.

Topper took the bottle from Asha and cracked a small smile at her.

Asha grinned back, “That wasn’t so hard, was it?” She asked.

“What?” Asked Topper.

“Smiling,” responded Asha, with the biggest smile on her face.

Topper handed back the water bottle, grunted, and looked away from the princess. He didn't want Asha to see his soft side, but Asha knew that he had one.

The two started to doze under the tree in the long grass, with the river flowing close by, sounding like a lullaby.

Large and colourful flowers blew over them in the light breeze as Asha and Topper fell into a deep slumber.

Chapter 8 - Kali

The sun was setting behind the mountains and the breeze was getting stronger. The grass blustered over Asha and Topper, who were still both asleep under the tree.

As the temperature of the air dropped, Asha woke-up.

The weather was changing, and it wasn't in a good way.

Asha gazed up at the sky to see the star path, but all that was visible were dark clouds. She could sense that something strange was happening, but she couldn't work out exactly what it was.

The princess stood-up to look around. She had a strange feeling in the pit of her stomach and it didn't feel good.

She walked over to Topper, who was still sound asleep, hidden in the long grass.

"Topper, Topper wake up," Asha said, gently putting her hand onto his shoulder to wake him.

Topper jumped to his feet startled and forgetting where he was for a moment.

“Why did you wake me up?” He said with a grumpy tone, “Never wake a sleeping elf!”.

“Do you feel the coldness in the air? There is something weird going on,” whispered Asha. “I have a strange feeling that something evil is coming.”

Topper looked around and walked over to the river. He tried to put his hand in the water, but it was frozen.

All of the flowers were closed, the grass was making angry wisps in the wind.

“There is darkness in the air, something definitely isn’t right,” said Topper. “We must continue to Agartha; our resting time is over.”

They gathered their things and headed over the river. They used the rocks poking out from the ice as stepping-stones.

Soon, the two of them had made it to the other side and were heading towards the next valley.

It was really dark, they didn't have the bright stars to help guide the way and to provide them with light. Every now and then as the dark clouds moved, they could just about see where they were going from the glimpses of light provided by the moon.

Asha and Topper walked towards the gap in between the two mountains and the clouds gave way to reveal more illumination.

Asha froze as she saw a dark shadow at the entrance of the alley way between the two mountains. This was the path that they needed to pass through to get to the entrance of Agartha.

Carefully, they crept closer to see what was standing in their path.

All of a sudden, Topper became very scared and shrunk behind Asha.

“Why are you hiding?” Whispered Asha.

“I have an eerie feeling about this creature who stands before us,” Topper whimpered.

“What happened to the bossy, ‘nobody can hurt me’ elf?” Asha whispered back at Topper.

“I was bluffing. I knew that you wouldn’t hurt me princess, you are the chosen one, the pure of heart blah blah blah,” he replied, forcing a smile at her despite his fear.

Asha looked back at Topper, scrunching up her face at the little elf, realising that he was very frightened of whatever was standing in front of them. She too had an eerie sense of dread about this beastly looking figure, but Asha never liked to judge. As a princess, Asha prided herself on always seeing the good in everyone and everything - until being proved otherwise of course!

“Okay, let’s take a deep breath and we can confront whoever it is standing in front of us,” whispered Asha to Topper.

"Whoever? You think it looks like a person?" Topper wailed.

"Sssshhhhh," Asha replied trying to calm him down.

Topper continued to hide behind Asha as she proceeded on towards the dark object standing in the distance.

Topper was shaking more as they moved closer. He had a far better view of the beast who was blocking the entrance to the next valley.

The creature had huge horns on its head, the face of a beast and the body of a muscular man.

He stood about twelve feet tall and his eyes were fiery red. His body was very dark and wrapped around him was a dragon. The dragon also had red eyes and very sharp looking teeth.

As Asha and Topper moved closer, they were both subjected to a very bad stench.

Asha thought to herself that, although she didn't know what death smelt like, she was pretty sure that it would be something close to this.

She stopped about twenty feet away from the beast and stared the evil looking creature down.

"We bring no harm to you," Asha shouted out.

The beast started to laugh, his long black pointy tongue poking out of his mouth. The dragon's head came out in front of the beast as if it were protecting him.

"Who are you and what do you want?" Asha asked.

"I am Lord Kali, I have come for my sword," he responded.

"I do not have your sword," Asha firmly said. "The Nandaka sword belongs to Kalki. It is my duty to return it to Shambhala for his arrival."

Kali laughed an evil laugh again and walked closer to Asha and Topper.

He stood above her and looked down at Asha whilst the dragon swooped behind Asha's back. Topper ran under a rock by the mountain and stood there trembling in fear of Kali and his dragon.

The dragon's scales scraped across Asha's back causing her to fall on her knees in front of Kali in pain. She looked up with anger in her eyes as he stared down upon her with an evil grin.

"I knew that you would bow down to me eventually, princess," Kali said, with an evil tone in his voice. "I can feel your anger towards me growing," he continued.

Kali took in a deep breath and laughed out loud, "Can't you just smell your own fear? It is intoxicating."

Asha closed her eyes to block out all of the bad energy that she felt Kali was trying to overpower her mind with.

She tightened her grip around the Nandaka sword and visualised nothing but love and kindness. Asha got up onto her feet and held the sword in front of her. Kali laughed again at Asha.

"You are nothing but a puny child. Do you really think that you can hurt me?" laughed Kali. "I will have that sword if I have to kill you to get it, princess."

Asha continued holding the sword in front of her pointing the sharp tip up towards Kali's neck. Kali became fiercer and small bursts of fire came from his red eyes.

"I am not here to fight you Kali, I just want to move past you peacefully. I will use this sword if I have to," said Asha.

"Do you really think you can defeat me?" Kali yelled out at the princess. "I am the ruler of this earth, nobody can defeat me," He replied as he reached to grab the Nandaka sword.

Asha edged backwards, still holding onto the sword as tightly as she could. She was feeling a little less confident as Kali stretched to full height, looking bigger and more fearsome.

"Love will always defeat the darkness Kali. You will not win this fight. I am the descendent of Krishna and I will fight evil to the end," Asha said with tenacity, regaining her confidence.

"You are nothing but a puny little human girl, who thinks that she has power because somebody told her that she is special," said Kali mockingly.

"You don't scare me," said Asha standing up tall to him. "I know that you can only hurt those who let you into their minds and their souls. You will never get into mine," she continued, remembering what the Jugal in the valley had told her about Kali.

Kali's skin turned darker and his eyes fierier as he got more and more angry.

He knew that what Asha was saying was true.

Kali may have been the Lord of the earth, but he wasn't the Lord of anyone that won't let him into their mind to control them. He was outraged that this child knew the secret to resisting him.

The angrier Kali grew, the angrier his dragon became also. Fire was pouring from the dragon's mouth. Asha stepped back so that she could avoid being burned.

Topper covered his eyes in fear as he watched this evil monster become fiercer.

"Asha, get out of there. You need to get away from him," Topper shouted out. "Kali may not be able to get into your mind, but fire is fire and you are still only a human," he cried out.

Asha had started to run away, with Topper following swiftly behind her. They ran back over to the other side of the frozen river. Kali ran after her still trying to get the Nandaka sword out of her hand.

Topper tripped on a rock and fell to the ground and Asha turned around to help him up. Kali hovered above them, reaching for the sword.

Asha stabbed at Kali and managed to get through his tough leathery skin, slicing into his hand.

Asha pulled on Topper's hand and rolled out from under Kali.

Asha and Topper ran as fast as they could to get away from Kali as he stared at his wounded hand. He truly seemed shocked and stunned that any young girl could bring him to harm, giving the princess and elf invaluable time to take the lead in their escape.

"We are going the wrong way to get to Agartha," Topper called out.

"What do you want me to do? Fly over him?" Asha replied with a sarcastic tone.

No sooner had Asha spoken when a gigantic bird flew down in front of them. Kali and his dragon were nearly caught up to them again, still trying to get the sword.

Kali grabbed onto Topper's cape that was flowing behind him.

"Stop resisting dwarf or I shall feed you to my dragon," Kali threatened in a deeper tone.

"Dwarf! I am not a Dwarf, I'm an elf," Topper angrily shouted back to Kali. Topper pulled his cape as hard as he could, tearing the bottom part that Kali was holding onto.

"My cape," Topper cried.

"I'll make you a new one, just run," Asha screamed out.

Topper was able to catch up to Asha, both running towards this gigantic bird.

"Get on its back," Topper demanded.

"Are you serious? How do we know that it isn't evil like Kali?" Asha questioned.

"Get on!" Topper shouted back. "It's Garuda, he was sent by the Gods to save us."

"How do you know?" Asha asked hesitant to get on its back.

"Do you really want to have this conversation now?" Topper said, throwing his hands in the air.

"Obviously I have met him before, trust me and get on, or stay here and die," Topper yelled back.

Asha and Topper climbed onto the gigantic bird and they flew up over the mountains. As they glided across the valley, they could hear the angry cries of Kali.

Garuda flew over into the next valley where Asha and Topper had been trying to travel to, but that had been blocked by Kali.

The grass was long and green again, the flowers were in full bloom and a waterfall was gushing down the rocks making the most serene sounds.

Asha petted Garuda on his head and thanked him for saving their lives and the sword.

Garuda flew off into the sky and Topper continued to lead the way towards Agartha.

Chapter 9 - Agartha

As the water gushed down the rocky mountain and the birds chirped a happy tune, Topper led Asha up the mountain, alongside the waterfall.

They reached a flat surface that followed the bends around the side of the mountain and into the cascading water.

As the travelling duo moved closer to the falling water, Topper was able to walk through, but Asha couldn't. For Asha, the water became solid like glass and wouldn't allow the princess to pass.

It was then that Asha remembered being told that she had to play the flute in order to prove that her heart was pure. The flute would only play a tune for those who were pure of heart.

She took the flute from her satchel and played the most beautiful tune. The music was so enchanting that the birds came down from their perches to sing with her.

The solid water barrier became soft and gentle and the falls opened up to allow princess Asha to walk through, like a goddess walking into her kingdom.

"Well, don't you get the royal treatment!" huffed Topper.

Asha shrugged back with a smile as they continued walking into the mountain. It was getting very dark as they proceeded deeper underground. Asha was worried about falling into a hole.

"Don't you have a light or something to see your way home?" Asha asked, feeling a bit unsure with Topper leading the way.

"Be patient Your Highness, let your heart lead the way," replied Topper.

"That's the first positive thing he's said since I've met him," murmured Asha to herself.

"What? Did you say something?" Topper asked.

"No, just talking to myself," answered Asha with a smile through the darkness.

They had walked through the cave for about an hour when Asha started to see a light shining through and she could hear the sound of water running.

Topper led Asha down steps that were carved out of the rock face. They walked towards water, where there was a small canoe tied to a post.

"Get in princess," Topper grumbled.

"You know Topper, it wouldn't hurt to smile once and a while," Asha said with a huge grin on her face. "We have just survived an attack from a pretty significant evil after all, and I'm sure that not many can make that claim. I for one am pretty happy that you weren't made into dragon soup!"

Topper grunted at the princess, climbed into the front of the boat, and grabbed an oar for himself. He handed a second oar to the princess.

"Sorry but you don't get the royal treatment here, you're going to have to help." He said.

As they rowed through the cave, the light in the distance became brighter.

Asha could see that it was made up from many different colors. She looked around to see where this light could be coming from and noticed luminescent plants glowing all around.

These plants were the most beautiful plants that she had ever seen, with so many different colors. There were purple, yellow, green, pink, blue shades and many others. Even the oversized mushrooms were glowing. It was like floating through a fairytale cavern.

As Asha stared at these giant mushrooms, she noticed something with wings peeking out from the side of one of them. She looked a little harder and could see that is was a fairy.

It was actually a bright green fairy that was about a foot tall with long white hair and pointy ears. The fairy's eyes were big and a glassy blue. In the dark they were as bright as the luminescent plants, which didn't make the fairies difficult to spot.

Asha gave a wave and a smile at the little fairy, who nervously waved back and flew away.

"They aren't used to humans being in Agartha," said Topper.

"Who?" Asha asked

"The fairies. Isn't that who you are waving to?" He asked. "They live just outside of the cave. They like to play in the plants and mushrooms all day and all night, play, play, play, that's all they do," Topper continued.

As they continued rowing through the magical cave, dozens of gigantic glowing yellow butterflies flew over their heads, and then back over their heads again.

"Another pest," grunted Topper.

"They are so beautiful," Asha said excitedly. Asha had loved butterflies since she was a little girl and to see some bigger than her and glowing in the dark had left her in awe.

As Asha continued to look around in amazement, she noticed huge crystals that seemed to be coming out of the rocks of the cave. The crystals glistened colors of the rainbow, reflecting back from all of the luminescent plants.

Everything just sparkled.

By this time, Asha and Topper were approaching the exit of the cave. Asha could see blue sky and a sun.

How could this be if we are inside the earth? She thought to herself.

In front of them on a little island was a very large tree - it was dazzling. The tree was so tall that it looked like it was touching the inner-earth sky.

As they got closer, Asha noticed that some of the branches were slowly falling off. This gave the princess an overwhelmingly profound feeling of sadness that she couldn't understand.

"That tree on the island, it's so lovely, yet I'm getting such a sad emotion from looking at it. Why is that?" Asha asked Topper.

"That is the tree of life. As outer earth continues to fall deeper into the age of Kali the tree loses a part of itself," said Topper.

"Will it grow back?" asked Asha.

"If or when mankind finally awakens and remembers where they came from it will," he responded. "Until then the tree will continue to weaken, as will Mother Nature on the outer earth. Mankind creating this destructive energy is like causing the walls of your own kingdom to crumble on top of yourself."

Asha took in a deep breath, she didn't realize how bad things were on the outside. *How could mankind have become so greedy and ignorant?* She thought.

As they passed the tree, Asha looked back at it once more to make a wish for a better future for her people. She closed her eyes to meditate so that she could regain her positive energy for the rest of her travels to Shambhala. She needed to move past this sadness.

"I will ask you again, aren't you too old to make wishes?" asked Topper.

"How did you know I made a wish?" Asha asked, surprised.

"You are in my world now and everybody who lives here is telepathic. That's why they call it the land of the peace, the land of silence. I can hear all of your thoughts," he explained.

I'm sure you can, my grumpy little friend. Have you even washed that beard lately? Asha thought to herself trying not to think mean thoughts about Topper.

"I heard that!" Topper shouted out.

Asha sunk into the boat some more, feeling embarrassed and trying really hard not to think of anything but pleasant thoughts. She looked around trying to concentrate on all the beauty that surrounded her.

The water was so pure that they could see the bottom of the river. The waterfalls looked a brilliant white as they gushed down.

The grass was greener than in her dreams and the air was at the perfect temperature, not too hot and not too cold. Everything was bigger, the birds, the fruit growing from the trees. The animals were at peace, there was no fear of being hunted by man or by other animals.

As they moved deeper into Agartha they entered into the first city.

A giant creature came out of the forest and made Asha jump.

She wasn't expecting to see anything like this. Asha recognized it as a troll from her studies when she was younger, although trolls were a myth and they weren't so big in her books back at home.

Asha thought to herself, *trolls are meant to be mean and greedy, so how did something of this nature end up in a place where only the pure of heart can enter?*

"I thought trolls were mean creatures?" asked Asha.

"You humans are always misunderstanding everything," Topper said, shaking his head. "Just because there is no beauty on the outside, you think something is mean, unkind or evil. Remember one thing princess, stop judging others! Evil can reside in the most beautiful being and in the most beautiful palace. Trolls were just misunderstood, so they came here to be free to roam without being persecuted, killed or displayed like an animal."

They continued down the river and under a bridge, where Asha saw a beautiful crystal palace. It looked like glass, shining so many different colors in the sunlight.

It was so beautiful that Asha could not stop staring at it.

“Is this Shambhala? Asha asked.

“No, this is the city of Posid. The Atlanteans came here when their island sunk into the Atlantic Ocean. Those who survived came to protect the remainder of their race from evil and greed that took over their land, just like Dwarka,” Topper responded.

Asha and Topper continued slowly down the gentle river, passing meadows with the most amazing beings that Asha had only seen in books of mythology.

She could see a beautiful white unicorn galloping free in the light breeze, with the long green grass brushing up against its legs as it passed by their canoe.

They passed villages with beautiful homes sitting on top of hills and mountains. The mountains didn’t have snow on top of them, because the temperature was always the same pleasant level of warmth in Agartha according to Topper.

As they passed one village they could see very tall, beautiful Agarthans sitting next to a waterfall, meditating together. Asha could feel their energy, so much so that she could hear music all around.

The music was so beautiful and peaceful that it reminded her of what she had heard when she called upon the Sea God in Gujarat.

This must be the music that the goddess Lakshmi was talking about, the music that is all around us, but we can only hear it when our consciousness is pure, Asha thought.

Asha stared at the beautiful giants as they rowed past, but not one of them noticed her. They were in deep meditation and completely oblivious to what was going on around them.

That is some serious dedication to meditation, Asha thought to herself.

Topper smiled seeing Asha's facial expressions and hearing her thoughts about all of the amazing and magical things in Agartha.

"It's unbelievable, isn't it?" Topper asked.

"Sorry, what? Did you say something?" Asha responded. She was too busy being mesmerized with all that was going on around her. She barely heard Topper talking to her.

"Agartha, it's unbelievable, isn't it?" he repeated himself.

"I never could dream of such a place, it's like a fairytale," Asha said, as she tried to pet a huge bird flying closely above them.

Topper took them under one more bridge. They were leaving the crystal city of Posid and entered into a huge lake that would take them into Shambhala.

As they rowed across the lake, Asha looked over the side of the canoe to see what was zipping by them with a whizzing noise and the occasional splash.

"There are large fish swimming all around us," Asha said out loud.

"Those aren't fish, they are mermaids and mermen," Topper responded.

Asha put her hand into the water to get their attention. One of the younger mermaids came out of the water, waved and smiled at her.

The Mer-people jumped in and out of the water around the canoe showing their playful side, welcoming the princess into their forbidden land.

"Everybody seems to be so happy and peaceful here," said Asha.

"That's because they know they aren't going to be captured or eaten by anything or anyone like they would be in the outside world," Topper said with a hint of sarcasm in his tone. "We are all vegetarians here, even the animals. There is no fear for survival because everything is plentiful in Agartha," he explained.

They continued across the lake, passing next to meadows and mountains. An assortment of different mythical creatures crossed their path.

One mythical creature that Asha didn't think she would see flying freely in Agartha was a dragon. She had never considered dragons to be peaceful creatures. Nonetheless, there a dragon was, flying out from one of the mountains in the distance. At first Asha thought it was a very large bird, but as it got closer she could see it was indeed a dragon.

Its leathery ocean blue skin sparkled in the sunlight, the gold on the top of its spikes glittered so much that it was blinding to the naked eye.

The dragon swooped down to the canoe and flew back up into the clouds.

Asha ducked her head and screamed. Topper laughed so hard at the princess that he nearly fell out of the canoe.

"Why are you laughing at me?" Asha asked.

"You should have seen your face," Topper said, still laughing at the princess.

"That dragon came for us and you sit here laughing," Asha shouted back at Topper.

"That dragon was playing with us. I already told you, nothing will hurt you here. We are all peaceful vegetarians, here to keep safe from the savages on the outside world," said Topper.

"Not all of us are savages," Asha mumbled.

"I can read your mind, Your Highness, you can mumble all you want I still know what you said," Topper said with a cheeky grin.

Asha looked up into the sky to see if she could see the dragon, but it wasn't there.

Suddenly the canoe sunk down a little in the stern and the bow lifted up out of the water. A shadow hovered behind Asha.

She very carefully turned around still feeling unsure. Sitting behind her was the dragon, looking playful and wanting some attention.

Asha put her hand up to its face to show the dragon that she wasn't a threat.

The dragon put its head in her hand and then gracefully flew into the sky again. The dragon soared around in the sky, and then disappeared over the mountains.

Topper sat and smiled at Asha, he could see why the Gods would pick her as the chosen one.

Her heart really is pure, he thought to himself. Topper could see in all of her actions, that Asha only saw the good in all that was around her.

The lake was becoming narrower as they headed into another crystal city.

There were more meadows with thousands of bees and butterflies flying around the beautiful flowers.

On the opposite side to the meadows, there were many hills and mountains with waterfalls that fed into the lake.

As they glided under a bridge, Asha could see another palace. This one was bigger and made up of crystals once again. The palace sat in the center of an adjoining lake with bridges on either side to cross onto the main land.

The residents of the city were much taller than Asha, with fair skin and huge blue eyes. Their skin was flawless, as was their hair. Their complexion looked light blue with sparkles, which reminded Asha of the stars shining at night.

The giant beautiful people stopped to stare at Asha and Topper as they rowed by.

The children waved excitedly at the princess. They had never seen a human from the outside world before.

"They seem to be in deep conversation without moving their lips. Does everyone just speak telepathically here?" asked Asha.

"Yes, all who live here have only good thoughts, so it doesn't matter who can hear them. It also takes more energy to talk. It's no wonder that you humans are so drained all the time, with all that gossiping," Topper said with a grin.

As the canoe floated closer to the crystal palace, Asha could hear that beautiful music again.

It sounds so peaceful, like Mother Nature singing to herself, Asha thought.

"It IS Mother Nature singing," said Topper reading her mind again.

"Is that where the music comes from, Mother Nature?" questioned Asha.

"Yes, when everything is in-sync with the mind, soul and body, the universe sings. Those who are in-sync with the universe can hear the music too," responded Topper.

He looked at Asha and smiled, then said pointing over to the Palace,

"Welcome to Shambhala, Princess Asha."

Chapter 10 - Shambhala

As Topper tied up the canoe, Asha noticed that there were two beautiful blue giant godly people standing above them at the dock. They were waiting to greet the princess and to take her into the palace to meet with their king and queen.

Asha couldn't stop staring at this race of beautiful people. She was fascinated with how their skin glistened like the crystals that surrounded them.

Asha disembarked the canoe and bowed. The beautiful female Agarthan pulled Asha to her feet and told her, "Asha you do not need to bow to us, we are all equals here."

"My name is Idalia and this is Aginor, please come inside with us, we can show you your quarters where you can rest. You must be exhausted!" she added.

Asha was exhausted, but she was too intrigued and excited with all that was going on around her to rest.

The three of them left Topper, walked into the palace and up the crystal stairs to Asha's quarters.

Half-way up the grand stairwell, Asha stopped and looked around in amazement.

Everything is so futuristic, like I've never seen before, thought Asha.

"We are thousands of years more advanced than the outside world," said Idalia.

I really have to stop having thoughts in my head, Asha thought. *Darn it, they can still hear your thoughts stupid!*

Asha was getting angry with herself and feeling really embarrassed.

Idalia and Aginor stood there staring at Asha, continuing to still hear the princess arguing with herself. She then looked up at them and smiled.

She felt awkward knowing that everybody in Shambhala could read her mind. Asha tried her hardest to just sing to herself instead.

After walking for a few minutes through long corridors, they finally reached Asha's room. They walked through two large crystalline doors that looked like dark tinted colored glass, to prevent people from looking through them.

The room looked so pure, everything was either made from crystals or white and blue materials.

It feels like I just walked into a human sized jewelry box, Asha thought to herself.

"That's because everything in Shambhala is made from earth stones," Idalia said to Asha.

"Sorry, I forgot that you can read my mind. I seem to be struggling with keeping my mind clear," Asha replied, feeling awkward again.

"You do not need to be sorry my child, we hold no judgement in Shambhala," Aginor assured her. "We will leave you in peace. Somebody will come for you this evening to take you to meet with the King and Queen," he continued, as they closed the crystal doors behind them.

Asha looked around her room and then she lay on her very comfortable white linen bed, trying to convince herself that she wasn't tired. She wanted to have the energy to go and explore this magnificent city.

Asha closed her eyes for a few minutes to absorb all of the sounds from outside of the castle.

She could hear birds chirping a happy tune and dragons swooping down and back up into the clouds again. Asha could hear horses running across the meadow.

The only thing that Asha couldn't hear were the voices of the people.

I would be so exhausted by the end of the day listening to the chitter-chatter in people's heads, she thought.

"We can choose what we want to hear princess, it just takes practice and discipline over time," Topper said as he struggled to open the gigantic crystal doors.

Asha jumped up with excitement and dashed over to help her little friend get inside.

"I'm so glad that you came up to see me, it's nice to see a familiar face," said Asha.

"I thought that you might want to have a look around. Actually, I heard it in your thoughts, that you wanted to look around. So here I am to escort you to wherever you want to go," expressed Topper.

"Thank you, thank you, thank you," Asha said, picking up Topper and hugging him.

"Okay, you can put me down now," Topper gasped in a grumpy tone. "Where would you like to start?" he asked.

"I would love to walk through the city and over to the meadows," Asha answered.

The two of them walked into the city and through the marketplace.

Asha saw the freshest fruit that she had ever seen. She stood there staring at what looked like a giant peach.

Asha had never seen anything like it. One of the blue people held out a peach for Asha to take.

"Thank you, but no thanks, I don't have any money," Asha said, looking at the delicious peach with a mouthwatering expression.

"We do not trade in Shambhala, anything you want is yours to take. The only rule we have is to never take our gems and rocks away from Shambhala. They are Mother Earth's natural resources and they are not meant to be used for greed and power," explained the blue giant lady who spoke so softly to Asha.

Asha smiled at the tall lady, took the peach and thanked her for being so kind and generous. Topper and Asha continued to walk through the marketplace, while Asha ate her peach. As she took her first bite the juice went all over her mouth.

“This is the best thing that I have ever eaten ever! It’s so juicy and so full of flavor,” Asha said, scoffing away at the fruit.

Topper looked up at Asha, trying not to grin at the mess that she was making by eating the peach. Asha looked at Topper’s face and they both burst into laughter.

“Princesses usually get their food cut up for them, so that they don’t make a mess of themselves,” said Asha.

Topper smiled back. He could see that Asha really felt free of judgement in Shambhala.

Topper took Asha over a crystal bridge to get to the meadow. It was so beautiful how the bridge glistened all the colors of a rainbow across the lake.

They stepped off the bridge into long green grass with many different colors and varieties of flowers growing. The grass felt so soft that Asha took her shoes off to run through it, before she fell down and rolled around.

In the distance, Asha could hear hooves stomping on the ground. She quickly got up to take a look. She could see a herd of white horses galloping past, heading towards the hills.

“Where are they going?” asked Asha.

"There is a resting area in one of the valleys of the mountains. There is a large fresh water lake for the horses to have a drink and to cool off," answered Topper.

"Are all of the horses wild here?" questioned Asha.

"Everything here lives in freedom. If an animal is needed, we ask them permission to take us where we need to go. We do not capture any animal in Shambhala, we are all equal," Topper responded in a slightly irritated tone.

"I will wait here, while you have a look around," said Topper.

Asha could feel that her sightseeing guide was not really accustomed to somebody as inquisitive as she was.

As she walked along the meadow, Asha deeply breathed in the fresh air and the smells of the flowers. She started to sense as though there was something familiar about her surroundings.

As Asha looked around, she could see a wooded forest on her left. Over to the right of her was a stream that connected to the lake.

All of this was as she had pictured in her dreams of the recent past.

The only thing missing was the voice of the beautiful lady that she had never been able to see. Asha always woke up before she was able to meet the person grabbing onto her shoulder.

"Asha, Asha my sweet child," a voice said.

And there it is, Asha thought to herself.

Before Asha could turn around, long blue fingers grabbed onto her shoulder just like in her dream.

For the first time, when Asha turned around there was actually somebody standing there.

Asha knew instinctively that it was the queen of Shambhala who had been haunting her dreams, and that it was the queen of Shambhala who was standing before her now.

The queen was absolutely magnificent, with her beautiful pure skin and long white hair. She was tall like the rest of the giant race living in Shambhala and had a beautiful crystal tiara with gems set inside of it on top of her head.

Asha knelt before her to pay her respects to the queen.

“Your Highness, it is an honor to meet you,” Asha said as she stood up.

“We are so glad that you made it to us, Princess Asha,” the queen replied. “We have waited thousands of years for this day to come.”

“The prophecy of me coming to Shambhala is thousands of years old?” questioned Asha. “Wow! That is a really long time. Who prophesized it?”

“I did!” said the queen.

“How is that possible? That would make you…” before Asha could finish her sentence the queen interrupted her.

“Thousands of years old,” said the queen with a gentle smile. “We came underground to keep ourselves pure. We have protected ourselves from evil and all that comes with evil, like disease. We have been able to control who comes in and who stays out,” said the queen, as she put her arm around Asha’s shoulders to guide her back towards the palace.

As they walked through the meadow the queen continued, “Visualize the earth like a human body. Mankind spends their whole lives focusing on what is on the outside of themselves rather than what is on the inside. This is the same way mankind looks at earth, they only see what's on the outside instead of understanding its inner core. This is how we have been able to stay sacred for thousands of years."

"If you don't let anyone in, then why did you choose me to come here?" asked Asha.

"My dear, sweet Asha, we did not choose you, you chose yourself," the queen answered.

Asha looked up at the queen feeling very confused with what she was telling her.

"I don't understand, how did I choose myself?" said Asha.

Before the queen could answer, Asha thought to herself, *I don't remember having a conversation with myself about being the chosen one.*

The queen chuckled at Asha's thoughts and clarified for the princess, "We all choose our destiny Asha, we all write our own story. Some have to rewrite their story until they get it right. Do you understand?"

Asha smiled at the queen as they continued to walk towards the palace. They caught up with Topper as he was picking flowers.

The queen stood above him, towering over him, staring, until he noticed that she was there.

"Your majesty," Topper said, as he bowed down to the queen and hid the flowers behind his back.

"Topper, you know that you are not supposed to pick the flowers," the queen said in a stern voice.

"I know Your Majesty, I'm really sorry. The thing is, I haven't been home in days because I was helping the princess get to Shambhala. I would like to give these flowers to my wife," Topper said hopelessly, looking up at the queen.

Asha started to feel guilty and responsible for the trouble that she had inadvertently caused for Topper with his family.

"Okay Topper, I will forgive you. Go and give the flowers to your wife, I will take Asha back to the palace to prepare for the festivities this evening," said the queen reverting back to her gentle voice.

Topper ran off with the bundle of flowers that he had just picked, while the Queen and Asha headed back to the palace.

Idalia and Aginor were waiting on the bridge for the queen and Asha's arrival.

"Princess Asha, may we escort you back to your quarters so that you can prepare yourself for the festivities this evening?" asked Idalia.

"I would like that very much, thank you," Asha said gratefully.

The three of them bowed to the queen and headed into the palace to get ready for this extraordinary event that Asha kept hearing about.

Asha walked into her room and found a beautiful long gown made of crystals waiting for her. Asha had never seen a gown like this before, it was very futuristic in her eyes.

"This gown is a gift for you from the queen. She would be honored if you would wear it to the festival tonight," said Idalia handing the dress to Asha.

"It's the most beautiful gown I have ever seen," Asha said with her eyes glistening from the sparkle in the dress. "We don't have anything like this where I come from."

"I'm glad that you like it, Your Highness. We will meet you downstairs in the grand foyer shortly," Idalia said graciously as she closed the doors.

Chapter 11 - The Festival

The festival was exactly as Asha had envisioned it. Everything sparkled as it should in her mind's eye, this was Shambhala after all!

The crystal city lit up the sky and everybody was celebrating. Asha wasn't too sure what they were celebrating for though.

After thousands of years, what is left to celebrate? Or is every day a celebration perhaps? She thought.

Asha's dress sparkled in the bright night. The princess glistened from top to bottom with her hair flowing down her back.

As Asha stood on the lower balcony looking over the hundreds of celebrating Agarthans, she was beginning to understand more than ever what the queen was trying to tell her. She was beginning to understand about the destruction of the external world that she lives in on a daily basis.

Being in Shambhala had given Asha a sense of inner peace. She really could sense that not one of the residents here had any envy or hatred in their hearts.

Asha didn't need to be telepathic to know this, she could just feel it.

As she looked around, all she could see and feel was happiness and love.

This is the way it should be in my world, Asha thought to herself.

As she stood there comparing worlds, the princess could see that, the more mankind became greedy for material possessions and for power, the uglier her world would become.

Why can't anyone see this? Asha thought.

"Because they have forgotten who they truly are," a voice said from behind.

"Your Majesty," Asha said as she bowed to the queen. "My apologies, I keep forgetting that you can read minds. Telepathy would be useful for me back at home, I would know when my parents are cross with me," Asha smiled cheekily.

"You could always look at their body language," replied the queen also with a grin.

They both stood for a moment in silence, watching the crowds as they enjoyed the festivities.

Asha broke the silence with a question, "What is this festival in honor of?"

"It is in honor of you, Asha," said the queen.

"Me? Why?" replied Asha. She was very curious as to why the people of this beautiful place would be celebrating her.

"Because you are the first of many chosen ones to finally reach Shambhala. Change is coming, and we must celebrate and embrace it," said the queen.

"There are more like me?" questioned Asha, suddenly not feeling quite as special.

"Not in your lifetime, but yes there will be many more to help change the world for the better. We call your kind the 'Light Workers'," the queen answered.

"What if I get things wrong and fail everybody?" asked Asha.

"Asha, in order to learn, you must make mistakes at times. You cannot fail anyone, we can only fail ourselves by giving up. When you first started to learn to walk, you stumbled many times, but you got back up and tried again. Think of going through life like a baby bird learning to fly, they don't give up. You must not give up!" The queen looked at Asha and smiled. "Now let us go and join in on the fun," the queen continued.

Everybody in the marketplace seemed to be having a good time, at least Asha thought they were from their body language.

They were all smiling at each other and some were dancing to the beautiful flute music. Other than for the music, it was the quietest festival she had ever been to. The people of Agartha were all communicating with one another Using telepathy. All except for Asha.

"Hello princess, I hope that you are enjoying the night," a deep voice said from below.

"Topper, I didn't think that this was your kind of thing," Asha said, looking down towards the elf.

"I guess you have grown on me princess," Topper said, trying to smile.

Asha smiled back at Topper knowing that in that small body of his, there was a big heart. *I guess when you are so small you have to act tough,* Asha thought to herself.

"I heard that," Topper shouted out to Asha as he led her into the marketplace.

"Damn this telepathy," Asha grumbled to herself.

As the evening drew to an end and many people had left the party, the queen came to Asha to bid her a good night

"Asha, we will have the ceremony in the morning," said the queen.

"Ceremony, what ceremony?" Asha asked.

"The passing of the Nandaka sword to the king," the queen responded.

"I almost forgot about the Nandaka sword, the whole reason I am here," Asha said, feeling embarrassed.

The queen left and headed back to the palace. Asha was left standing in the Marketplace alone.

As she was about to leave, the baby blue dragon from earlier flew down in front of her. He bowed his head so that she could pet him.

"Aren't you the cutest dragon I've ever seen," Asha said whilst rubbing his head. "Although I guess that you're the only good dragon I've ever seen," Asha mumbled under her breath.

The dragon flew off and Asha headed up to her room to get some sleep.

As Asha walked into the palace she couldn't help but wonder why that dragon was so interested in her.

"It's because you both have a connection with the sword," a voice came from behind.

"Idalia, I didn't realise anybody was behind me," Asha said. "How do we have a connection with the sword?" Asha asked.

"You are the chosen one to deliver the sword, and the breath of that dragon will be used to make it powerful enough to destroy the darkness," explained Idalia.

"When will all of this happen?" Asha asked.

"We don't know, but it won't be for a very long time, maybe even thousands of years. It all depends on how quickly the external world becomes completely evil and dark," said Idalia. "If we can save your world from the darkness, we won't need the sword."

"I thought it was already foreseen?" Asha asked.

"It has been prophesized, but prophecies can change. That is where the 'Light Workers' come in. We must always remember that even in the darkest times, the darkness can always move into the light," said Idalia with so much compassion. "You must understand Asha that we are all writing our own stories, and only we can change them. There are some, like yourself, that chose to be here to help guide the lost back into the light, but it is up to us and only us to create our own destinies. We must have faith that love will win in the end."

"If people are not born evil, then why do some choose it?" questioned Asha wanting to understand more.

"Some who desire material items become possessed with wanting more. Some never feel as though they have enough, so they will do anything to get more and more. In the external world, the more you have, the more power you have over other people. It then becomes a greed that takes over their hearts and darkens them," answered Idalia.

"So, in order to know love, we must be poor?" said Asha feeling very confused.

"Not at all, Your Highness. Look around you! Everything here is made from the earth. The crystals, the waterfalls, the meadows and all of the gems have come from Mother Nature. We all use these earthly materials, but we do not desire them, we respect them. We do not have greed or envy in our hearts. You must be successful in all you do, but never have attachments. I wasn't born with gold in my hands and I will not leave this planet with gold in my hands, the gold will be passed on," Idalia said.

"I think I'm beginning to understand. Thank you!" said Asha, as she bid Idalia a good night, and went to her room to get some sleep before the ceremony in the morning.

Chapter 12 - The Ceremony

It was a beautiful morning in Shambhala as was usual and expected.

I suppose the weather stays exactly the same temperature every day, so there is never any bad weather, Asha thought to herself.

The princess woke up feeling wide-eyed and refreshed from a good night of sleep. She got out of bed and walked over to a round ottoman, where she had laid down the sword the day she had arrived. Asha held it in her hands, staring at it.

Today was going to be her last day in Shambhala, the day she was handing over this sacred artifact to the king.

Even though Asha missed her parents, Najeena and of course her friend Aadesh, she was really going to miss Shambhala and her new friends here. Most of all she was going to miss how peaceful it was.

The time quickly came for Asha to get ready and to head to the throne room for the ceremony.

Asha buffed the sword with the cloth that she had kept it in and went downstairs to the grand foyer, where everyone was congregating until they were called into the throne room.

It looked as though the whole of Agartha was present, including Topper and his wife.

The guards opened the large doors to the throne room and invited the crowd in to be seated.

Asha was asked to stand at the doors until the king and queen called for her.

She felt quite uneasy with the whole process because nothing was rehearsed, as she was accustomed to for such ceremonies. She didn't know what to say or do.

"Excuse me Sir," Asha called out to one of the guards. "I'm not quite sure what I'm meant to be doing."

"The king is about to speak so we must be quiet," said the guard to Asha.

I really hope I don't mess the ceremony up, Asha thought to herself.

"You'll be fine, Your Highness. You will walk down the aisle to the king and queen, and you will simply kneel before them, holding the sword out in both hands," a voice said coming from behind.

"Idalia, thank goodness. I was really scared for a moment, I actually would have thought about running away," responded Asha, "if it wasn't for the fact that everybody would have telepathically heard me think about running away, which wouldn't have gone down very well I would imagine!" Asha shone her signature grin to her new friend.

"Come, let's be ready for when the king calls for you," Idalia said, smiling back at Asha.

Idalia and Asha stood in the doorway waiting to be called. A flute player started to play music and Idalia led the way towards the King and queen with Asha following.

When they reached the thrones, Asha knelt and held the sword out in front of her. The king and queen stood up and walked over to Asha.

"We have gathered here today to receive the Nandaka sword from the chosen one, Princess Asha. This sword represents the start of a new age and the end of the darkness we know as Kali Yuga," the king preached to his people. "There will come a time when we all will be living in peace and the darkness will find the light or perish. This Sword represents purity, knowledge and wisdom. It will be the destroyer of ignorance!" The king shouted out to his people.

The crowd cheered at the king's speech. As the cheers subsided, he calmed the congregation to continue with the ceremony.

"Princess Asha, you have come a long way to bring us the Nandaka sword. The world will one day be indebted to you for your courage and devotion to enlighten the external world."

The king took the sword from Asha's hands and walked over to the dragon that Asha had befriended the night before. The dragon breathed fire onto the sword until it glowed, and the king plunged the blade into a giant piece of crystal.

"This sword will stay within this rock until the birth of Kalki. Until then, we will continue to fight the darkness and know that good will always triumph," said the king.

Everyone cheered and clapped for their king and Princess Asha, there was now hope for the people on outer earth. Asha felt more at ease knowing that one day Kalki would be born to fight the darkness and finally end the war of good versus evil.

Goodness will one day prevail for all.

After the ceremony, the people of Shambhala gathered in the city center to continue enjoying the festival. Princess Asha joined in the festivities for her last day, before her upcoming return to the kingdom of Panchala.

As Asha walked around to mingle and to say her goodbyes, she was rejoiced by the people with gifts of various sumptuous fruits.

A giant blonde man had made her a tiara out of crystal with beautiful sapphires. He said that the sapphires represented the goodness of Asha's soul and put it onto her head.

"Do not worry Princess Asha, I have been given special permission by the queen for you to take this gift away with you," said the man.

As Asha's face gleamed with happiness and peace, her eyes filled with tears of sadness. Shambhala now held a very special place in her heart, and she realized that she may never see this place or its people again.

"It is better to have known, even for a short while, than to never have known at all," said the queen walking towards Asha.

"Even though I've only been here for a short while, this feels like home. I'm really going to miss being here," Asha said sadly, wiping a tear from her cheek.

"My dear princess, you are a part of us now. All you have to do is close your eyes and meditate. If you think of us, if you think of Shambhala, you will be here. You have the power, you just need to believe in yourself," said the queen.

They hugged each other tightly and joined the crowd for the final hour of festivities. It was getting dark and the crowds were becoming smaller as the revelers returned to their homes.

Eventually, only Asha and Topper remained.

"So, I guess you are going to need me to take you back out of Agartha," Topper grumbled.

"It would be nice if you could do that for me," responded Asha, smiling down at the elf. "I think I will retire for the night and get a good night of sleep. See you in the morning, Topper."

Chapter 13 - The Final Day

Princess Asha woke-up hearing a commotion, after an incredibly restful night of sleep. She walked over to the window to see what was going on outside.

Shambhala had not been at all noisy since she had arrived, given that the residents were all telepathic, but today was different for some reason.

Asha quickly dressed and rushed to see what the fuss was all about.

Idalia and Aginor were having a very serious discussion with the queen close to the dock, where Topper was in the process of tying up his canoe.

As Asha approached, the party became quiet and started to speak telepathically to prevent her from hearing their conversation.

“Good morning!” Asha said as she curtseyed to the queen. “Is everything okay?” she asked.

The queen put her hands onto Asha’s shoulders, “Everything is fine, there is nothing for you to worry about. Idalia has packed some fruit for your journey home.”

Idalia handed the wrapped-up fruit to Asha and gave her a hug goodbye. “We will all miss you Princess

Asha. You are now family to us and we will always be here for your protection," Idalia said with a sadness in her voice.

Aginor bowed to the princess, "the whole world will one day know of who you are and of your courage." He added.

"And so say we all!" said the queen. "We still have a long and hard battle ahead of us, but you must remember, no matter how hard the fight is, good always wins. We may not always win the battles, but we will win the war. Asha please remember, always follow the stars to help guide you home if it becomes too dark. There will always be light to lead the way."

Asha hugged the queen goodbye and Aginor helped her onto the canoe.

Topper pushed the canoe away from the dock with his oar and headed under the crystal bridge. Crowds had gathered on the bridge with hundreds of people waving goodbye to Asha as she rowed with Topper across the lake.

"The darkness has become worse, Your Majesty. We should have warned the princess, so that she could prepare herself for when she arrives back onto the outer earth," Adalia said to the queen telepathically.

"Princess Asha is very powerful. She has more power than she knows or understands. We cannot interfere with this power or the outside world. This is a part of her journey, the prophecy must not be tampered with," replied the queen.

The white unicorn was running across the meadow with horses following behind.

The blue dragon flew across the path of Asha and Topper. He landed on the bow of the canoe to say his goodbyes as well. Asha petted his head and he flew off into the mountains behind them.

As they passed through the other cities, the people were going about their business as usual. Some were meditating to the sounds of the flutes and the waterfalls.

As they moved closer to the cave exit, Asha could see the fairies looking cautiously from behind the very large mushrooms, watching the princess pass through their home once again.

Just before they reached the entrance of the cave, a young fairy girl flew over to Asha and gave her a flower before quickly flying away.

"Your heart must be the purest, fairies never come that close to anyone," Topper said.

Topper rowed the canoe up to the dock and tied it to a post. He jumped onto the dock then helped Asha to climb out of the canoe.

Topper led the way up the steps that were carved out of the rockface. The two of them were very quiet as they journeyed towards the entrance to Agartha.

As they reached the top of the cave, they both stood in front of the waterfall and stared at each other.

"I guess this is goodbye," grumbled Topper.

"I guess so. Are you going to miss me?" asked Asha.

Topper spurted out a laugh, then looked up at Asha who was pulling a face at him.

"Oh, you were serious," he said.

Topper laughed again, came closer to Asha and gave her a hug, "of course I'm going to miss you."

Asha bent down to hug him back and thought to herself,

Okay there Mr. Grumpy Pants, you can let go now.

"I can still hear your thoughts, princess," Topper blurted out. They both stopped hugging each other and laughed to mask the sadness that they were both feeling.

Asha knew that emotions were very difficult for Topper. She respected him and his strange qualities.

Asha headed through the waterfall and back out onto the Himalayan Mountains.

As she walked down the side of the mountain, the princess turned around to say her last goodbye to Topper.

Asha could see him standing behind the waterfall, waving as the water got thicker and thicker until he disappeared.

Asha's adventures in Shambhala were over.

As she continued to walk down the mountain, she thought to herself, *will I wake up tomorrow morning and these amazing experiences will all feel like a dream?*

Chapter 14 - Home Sweet Home

Asha finally reached the ground and headed through the first of many valleys towards her own kingdom.

As she was walking along the valley, she noticed that everything seemed very quiet, a bit too quiet and eerie. Something didn't seem right, not even the birds were chirping.

Asha hurried along to get to the next valley to see if anything had changed from how she remembered as she moved further away from Agartha.

It was worse! Asha ran as quickly as she could to get to the village in the valley where the Jugal and his family lived, who were so kind to her on her way through previously.

Maybe I can get some answers there, Asha thought.

Asha reached the river that ran in front of the village, but there was barely any water running through it.

Asha jumped across some stones that were sticking out of what was left of the river and ran across the field to the cottage.

Just as she was about to knock on the door, it opened. It was Jugal's wife and she had tears rolling down her cheeks.

"What is the matter?" asked Asha. The farmer's wife opened the door wide to let Asha in to see Jugal. He was lying in a bed, very weak and sick. Asha knelt at his bedside.

Jugal whispered to Asha, "You must hurry home, the darkness is taking over, people are becoming very sick and many are dying."

All Asha could think about was her parents and Aadesh, *what if they are sick, or worse?*

Asha turned to Jugal's wife, "What has caused this, what has changed since I have been gone? It has only been a few days."

"Your Highness, you have been gone for months, not days," replied the farmer's wife.

"That can't be, I only spent two nights in Shambhala. This doesn't make any sense," Asha said feeling distressed and confused.

Jugal called Asha over in a weak voice, "Legends say that time is not the same in Shambhala as it is out here. While you were gone, Kali has moved to take over, you must defeat him and save us all princess."

Asha nodded her head to her friend. She said farewell to the farmer and his family and collected her belongings.

Just as she was leaving, a healer walked into the cottage.

"Please take care of him, please make sure that he gets well," Asha said to the healer. The healer nodded his head and walked over to the bedside.

Asha took one last look at Jugal and saw him wave with all the energy he had left in him. She waved back, smiled with uncertainty and left for her own kingdom.

As she walked across the fields of the valleys, all she could think about was her kingdom, her family and how they must be despairing with her being away for so long.

Asha dreaded to think what might have happened to them if Kali's darkness had taken over the Kingdom of Panchala.

Asha ran from valley to valley trying to make her way home as quickly as possible, but the darkness seemed to be getting worse and worse.

It felt like Mother Earth was angry at mankind and was trying to teach a lesson.

How did this happen so quickly? Asha thought to herself.

Asha remembered the Queen of Shambhala speaking about the darkness, and how it will get worse before it gets better. She didn't think it would all happen so fast.

As the night drew closer and the skies became darker, she remembered the queen speaking about using the stars to find the light.

Asha pressed on until she made it out of the mountains. She was out of breath and exhausted, but she knew that she must continue.

The princess walked along the fields, trying to determine what she was supposed to do to stop the darkness.

In the distance, she saw a beautiful black horse with a white mane and tail grazing in the fields. Asha got closer to take a better look at this stunning horse that looked so familiar.

"Spirit!" Asha shouted out. Spirit looked up, trotted over to Asha and nestled his head into her arms. "I can't believe it's you. What are you doing out here all alone?

I'm not sure why I just asked you that, it's not like you can answer me. Asha thought.

"We are here looking for you," a voice calmly said from behind.

Asha turned around to see who the familiar voice was, "Aadesh, is that really you?" Asha squealed with excitement and ran over to her favorite farmer and friend. Aadesh dismounted his horse to hug the princess.

"Why are you out here looking for me?" Asha asked. "Is it my parents? Najeena?"

"All is okay with your parents and Najeena, you must calm yourself princess. You have been gone for quite a while, the nature of your journey I would imagine. I had a dream and had to come and find you. Your parents had given up hope of your safe return to the kingdom," Aadesh said sadly. "Things are not good here; the people of the kingdom and many other kingdoms have given up hope. Theft and greed have become normal to mankind. Gambling and crimes have now hit our kingdom and many other kingdoms around India. People are going mad, they no longer recognize what is wrong or right. Disease is killing more and more people, it has become an epidemic. Come, let's get you back to your very concerned parents. I wish to hear of your adventures."

Aadesh helped Asha onto Spirit and they galloped over to the fields towards the Kingdom of Panchala.

After hours of riding over fields and pastures, they arrived into the kingdom and rode through the city.

Asha looked in astonishment at how much everything had changed in so little time.

People were fighting over gold and arguing with one another. This was not the Panchala that she had left before she journeyed to Shambhala.

"All that I have done, the journeys I have taken to save my people from this evil, has this all been for nothing?" Asha said sadly.

"Asha, this is not your fault! This is the karma that these people have brought upon themselves," Aadesh said sternly.

"I was meant to stop this from happening, that was to be my destiny, I am the chosen one," Asha continued.

"You are the chosen one to help awaken consciousness to guide us to enlightenment. It is up to us as individuals to make the changes to become better people. Humans have failed to follow their hearts and instead follow minds that are broken and sick. Humanity will lose its place in the world and will live in oblivion within the darkness," Aadesh paused and continued thoughtfully,

"Some will follow their hearts and remember their divine roots and join the fight to end the age of Kali. You, my dear princess, planted the seed. It is up to humanity to water it and to let it grow," Aadesh stated.

"So how do we fight against a darkness that has no flesh? How can we take our men to war to destroy something that cannot be seen?" asked Asha.

"The war against the darkness is symbolic, Asha. It will not be a physical fight but one from the heart. We must continue to raise consciousness with mankind, help them to remember where they came from, to help them be rid of their demonic tendencies. When we take on this fight, those who are still pure must always remember who they are and must not get lost in the darkness." Aadesh replied.

Asha rode the rest of the journey home in silence, taking in all that she had seen, and all that Aadesh had said.

The king and queen were standing outside on the grand staircase of the palace, waiting for their precious princess to come home.

As Asha and Aadesh rode into the gates of the palace, Asha jumped down from Spirit's saddle before he even came to a halt. She ran to her mother and father as fast as she could.

The Queen cried as she held her baby girl in her arms for the first time in months. The king thanked

Aadesh for bringing his daughter home safely, then went over to join in the reunion with his daughter. While Asha and her parents were hugging, a cold wet nose pushed in underneath the three of them.

"Najeena," wailed the princess as she hugged her pet cow.

The royal family and Najeena went into the palace to fetch a meal for the hungry princess.

"Prince Emir will be here in the morning," said the queen to Asha.

"I'm surprised he isn't here already," Asha said, with a mouthful of food.

"The kingdom of Gujarat is having many problems with their people. He needed to attend to them before he left to come here. This darkness has reached everywhere in India," the queen replied.

"What is going to happen to us? The mind is a powerful thing. How can we fight it?" questioned Asha.

"So is the heart, Asha. The darkness of Kali is disconnecting the mind from the heart, we just need to help the people connect the two together again," the queen answered.

"You must not concern yourself with this today, you need your rest. Even the chosen one must sleep." The queen walked Asha to her room and helped her into bed, kissed her on the forehead and bid her goodnight.

"Mother," Asha called out before the queen closed the door.

"What is it my sweet child?"

"I will fix this, I will get rid of the darkness," Asha said.

"I know that you will my darling." The queen blew a kiss to Asha and closed the door, so that Asha could get some rest.

In the morning, when Asha woke up, she noticed that the sun wasn't shining as brightly into her window as it did before her journey.

The darkness is affecting Mother Earth just as it was predicted, Asha thought. Life was changing for everyone, and it wasn't for the better.

Asha went to get ready for breakfast. As she was putting on her red and gold sari that Prince Emir had gifted her, she could hear the sound of horse hooves trotting through the palace gates.

"It's Emir," Asha shouted out loud. She hurriedly put on the sari and ran downstairs to greet the man with whom she was falling in love.

Asha ran outside and down the grand courtyard steps, tripping up over her own feet. Luckily, she fell into the arms of her prince.

"Easy, Your Highness. I like looking at that pretty face, I don't want to see it hit the floor!" smiled Prince Emir, as he helped put Asha's two feet back onto the ground.

Asha blushed with embarrassment. She didn't like making a fool of herself, especially in front of the prince.

"I'm so glad that you are here, everything is going to be so much brighter now. I can feel it!" said Asha.

The young royals walked into the palace to have breakfast with the king and queen.

Asha and Emir couldn't stop smiling at each other. It was like the darkness didn't even exist for Asha, and everything was blissful with the world.

"Asha, you must tell me what the people of Shambhala said to you about Kali Yuga. How are we supposed to fight the darkness?" asked Emir.

"The queen didn't say much about fighting the darkness, she just told me that it will get worse for all of us, and that there is more work to be done before it will get better. The queen did say that we cannot fight the darkness physically. It is a fight that must be undertaken with the heart, mind and the soul." Asha explained.

"Asha, there is something I must tell you," Emir said to Asha with a concerned look on his face.

"What is it Emir? Is there something wrong?" asked Asha.

"I went back over to Dwarka to see if I could find anything ancient and with meaning that our ancestors left behind," said Emir.

"And, did you find anything?" Asha asked, feeling nervous of the answer she was about to receive.

"There were twelve very large crystals, they look like they were meant to connect with something, but we are not sure with what. We have put these crystals under guard so that nobody can get near to them. We need to find out what these crystals were used for and why," said Emir.

"In Shambhala they used crystals for everything, even to build with. They were a source of energy for the inhabitants. Maybe Krishna did the same for his Kingdom of Dwarka," Asha said in a hesitant tone.

"Yes, this could be true. Nevertheless, we will keep the crystals guarded until we know what we are meant to do with them," confirmed Emir. "Now that we have discussed this business, it is time for some fun!" Emir said with some excitement in his tone. "What shall we do today, my beautiful princess?"

“We could go to the farm. I could introduce you to my friend Aadesh and he can teach you how to milk cows,” smiled Asha from ear to ear.

“Milk cows!” Emir said pulling a face at Asha. “We are royalty Asha, we do not milk cows.”

“Prince Emir, you must humble yourself and learn to become one with nature. It is most enlightening,” Asha said firmly. “It’s also therapeutic and a lot of fun. Besides, Krishna was a God, didn’t he herd and milk cows?” said Asha in a softer tone.

“Okay, you have me there. For you Asha, I will learn how to milk cows,” Emir said grinning at his princess.

Prince Emir called for his horse and for Asha's as well.

Asha quickly stopped him. "In order to experience nature properly, we must walk."

Emir rolled his eyes at the princess and reluctantly followed behind her and little Najeena as they walked out of the palace gates.

"You are lucky that I love you," Emir softly whispered to Asha.

Asha smiled from ear to ear, not quite sure what to say. Of course, she loved the prince, but she wasn't sure if she was ready to tell him that she loved him.

Asha continued walking, pretending that she didn't hear him.

As they walked through the marketplace, Emir and Asha saw and felt that things were changing. The energy from the people was becoming negative.

They saw several incidents of unnecessary hostility. Greed and hatred were surely taking over.

Asha and Emir hurried through the markets and over the fields to Aadesh's barn. Aadesh had already herded the cows into their stalls to prepare them for milking.

"It seems that we are just in time," Asha said, as she walked into the barn with Najeena trotting beside her. Emir was walking behind them, making another face at her.

"Princess Asha, what a pleasant surprise. This must be Prince Emir," Aadesh said as he bowed to the prince. "Is this a friendly visit or are you here to collect some milk?"

"We are here to milk the cows with you, Aadesh," Asha excitedly said, whilst looking at Emir's face.

"What perfect timing," Aadesh said, amused at the young royals and their body language towards each other.

It was a long afternoon milking the cows at the farm. It was getting dark and time to retire for the evening.

Prince Emir escorted Asha back to the palace and to her room, so that he could wish her a good night in private.

Prince Emir opened the princess's bedroom doors and then pulled her closer to him for a good night kiss. Asha blushed as usual and was left standing speechless as the prince smiled, bowed and walked to his own quarters to get some rest.

Epilogue

It was the middle of the night and Asha found herself once again standing in the meadow of Shambhala, only this time it was different. She could actually see the Queen standing in front of her.

"Asha, you must understand that you cannot wake mankind up and bring them out of the darkness, you can only shine the light to help them see. Each person is responsible for their own journey in life, one cannot purify another. This is not the first cycle of the Kali Yuga and it will not be the last. It is time for you to awaken Atlantis, it is time to start the process of the new Golden Age," said the queen.

Asha woke up startled, with sweat rolling down her forehead as it did every time she had these dreams.

"Atlantis? I thought Atlantis was just a fairytale," Asha whispered to herself.

That same night in the deep ocean of the South Atlantic, between Africa and South America, were twelve very large and powerful crystals. Each crystal was set in a corner of a forgotten city. The crystals started to light up and cause tremors along the bottom of the ocean. The walls of the long-lost city began to shake.

The tremors were so strong that even the earth began to move, even as far as the kingdom of Panchala felt the earth move.

As Asha sat on her trembling bed she knew it was time to take on her toughest quest yet to save mankind.

--- THE END ---

www.ingramcontent.com/pod-product-compliance
Lightning Source LLC
Chambersburg PA
CBHW071145170626
46809CB00002B/771
9781999602055